MASTER

Perhaps Jessica was making a dreadful mistake in marrying Craig Stafford; for although she loved him she knew only too well that his only reason for marrying her was that he wanted a son. Yet in that case, why on earth hadn't he proposed to Caroline Paige instead?

Books you will enjoy by KAY THORPE

A MAN OF MEANS

Although Mark Senior was so much older than she was, and an experienced, wealthy man of the world, Dana was in no doubt that she wanted to marry him—and not just for his money! But even after they were married Mark continued to treat her as if she were a child—so perhaps it was not surprising that she should turn to his younger brother Brendon...

THE NEW OWNER

Sculla, the tiny island off the Cornish coast, had been a happy home for Thea all her life, and with her impending marriage to Gavin Grant it would continue to be her home for ever. Or so she thought—before David Barrington came storming on to the scene, to change everyone's lives for better or for worse!

TEMPORARY MARRIAGE

Regan had just five weeks to find herself a husband, or lose her home, and when Keir Anderson turned up out of the blue—and out of her past—she asked him to marry her, as a purely temporary, business affair; and Keir agreed. But then he proceeded to turn the tables on her... not once, but twice!

COPPER LAKE

For love of a man Toni had come from England to Canada—but he had deceived her and let her down, which was how she now came to be working in British Columbia for Rafe and Sean Stewart. And now everything and everyone was conspiring to get her engaged to Sean, despite the fact that she didn't love him nor he her. Which made it doubly unfair that as a result Rafe should develop the worst possible opinion of her!

MASTER OF MORLEY

BY
KAY THORPE

MILLS & BOON LIMITED
15–16 BROOK'S MEWS
LONDON W1A 1DR

All the characters in this book have no existence outside the imagination of the Author, and have no relation whatsoever to anyone bearing the same name or names. They are not even distantly inspired by any individual known or unknown to the Author, and all the incidents are pure invention.

The text of this publication or any part thereof may not be reproduced or transmitted in any form or by any means, electronic or mechanical, including photocopying, recording, storage in an information retrieval system, or otherwise, without the written permission of the publisher.

This book is sold subject to the condition that it shall not, by way of trade or otherwise, be lent, resold, hired out or otherwise circulated without the prior consent of the publisher in any form of binding or cover other than that in which it is published and without a similar condition including this condition being imposed on the subsequent purchaser.

First published 1983
Australian copyright 1983
Philippine copyright 1983
This edition 1983

© Kay Thorpe 1983

ISBN 0 263 74220 2

set in Monophoto Times 10 on 11 pt.
01-0483 – 57145

Made and printed in Great Britain by
Richard Clay (The Chaucer Press) Ltd,
Bungay, Suffolk

CHAPTER ONE

THE sun was shining when Jessica awoke, yesterday's grey skies and drizzling rain a thing of the past.

She stretched luxuriously in the double bed, conscious of a new lightness of mood as she contemplated the day ahead. With only herself to please she could either stay on here in Harrogate for a while or carry on farther afield. This touring holiday had been a good idea in that it left room for flexibility. A break from routine of any kind was what she had needed.

Getting out of bed, she crossed to the window, drawing back the woven curtains on a view of gracious old buildings and flower-strewn gardens. Time had, to a great extent, stood still in this part of the world. Top hats and long, sweeping dresses would not have looked at all out of place on the street down there.

The thought of top hats brought a swift little pang, just as swiftly squashed. Brian had been right: marriage wasn't the right answer for them. Their relationship lacked that essential ingredient. A clean break was best for them both. Changing her job was a part of that same desire for a new start. Life had to have more to offer than nine to five boredom—not that she had anything else lined up as yet. Time enough to think about that when she got back from this break. Perhaps she might even consider working overseas for a spell. Trained secretaries were in great demand, by all accounts. At twenty-three, with no family commitments, she was in a position to do whatever she felt like doing. There was some consolation in that.

Dressed in cream linen slacks and matching shirt, she made her way downstairs to the dining room, stopping by at the desk on the way to extend her stay over the weekend. The town would make a good centre from which to explore the surrounding countryside, and she would still have four days left to travel east to York and the coast as she had planned. Whether she would actually seek out the Stafford place remained to be seen, and even if she did it would only be to view it. One didn't burst in on total strangers to announce a relationship as tenuous as hers.

Breakfast was excellent, if a little more substantial than she was accustomed to. Over a second cup of coffee, she took out her 'Guide to the Dales' in order to plan her day, tracing a route out along the A59. This morning she would spend right here in Harrogate looking around the town, this afternoon she would visit Skipton. Tomorrow depended very much on how she felt about things.

After a moment or two she gave way to temptation and turned the pages to the chapter on places of historic interest again. There were photographs of several, including one of a lovely, gracious old manor house set against a background of hills. Morley Grange, home of the Stafford family for more than two hundred years, said the accompanying legend. How could Grandmother have found it in herself to give up all that? Jessica wondered, not for the first time. Could love ever really compensate for the loss of one's family? The marriage had been a happy one, true, but there must have been regrets.

Sitting there, she cast her mind back over what little she knew of the story, trying to put herself in her grandmother's shoes. Emma Stafford had been just eighteen when she had run away from home with the chauffeur's son, and her father had never forgiven her for marrying below her station. On his death there had been no mention of a daughter in his will.

Jessica's mother had been the only child of that

marriage, as Jessica herself was an only child. Had there been a brother or a sister the death of her parents in a car crash three years ago might have been a little easier to bear. Being left almost entirely alone in the world at twenty was no joke. Many had been the time she had contemplated getting in touch with her cousins, but that was as far as she had got. Even now she had little intention of doing more than take a look for curiosity's sake. Any closer approach could so easily be misconstrued, and she would hate it to be imagined she was looking for any handouts on the strength of family ties.

'Do you mind if I share your table?' asked a male voice, jerking her out of her introspection, and she looked up to find a fair-haired young man smiling down at her from behind the far chair. 'All the others appear to be taken,' he added apologetically.

Jessica returned the smile, liking his clean-cut looks. 'That's all right. I was about ready to leave anyway.'

'Oh, don't rush off,' he exclaimed, sliding into the chair. 'Stay and have another coffee at least.' His smile widened disarmingly. 'I only chose this table because you were sitting here. If you leave now I'm going to feel distinctly slighted.' He held out a long-fingered, brown hand. 'Peter Turner. I'm a local G.P., if that's any reassurance.'

'It's a very adequate testimonial,' Jessica agreed, relaxing to his easy manner. 'I'm Jessica Chappel. Do you usually come here for breakfast?'

'I had an early call, and home is the other side of town,' he said. 'Anyway, my mother is away and Dad will already have eaten.'

'Is he a doctor too?'

'That's right. We share a practice—at least, we shall eventually, when people round here learn to trust the word of a young upstart fresh out of medical school.' His grimace was wryly good-natured. 'I've been qualified for more than a year in actual fact, but most still ask to see my father.'

That would make him around twenty-six, Jessica conjectured. He looked younger, which couldn't be much of a help. Boyish enthusiasm was a somewhat inadequate substitute for a cultivated bedside manner.

'I imagine they'll adjust eventually,' she said. 'They'll have to, won't they?'

'Sure.' His tone was dry. 'By the time Dad's ready to retire I should be getting through.' He paused there, hazel eyes frankly appraising her fine, regular features under the pale fall of red-gold hair. 'What brings a girl like you to our part of the country?'

'I'm on holiday,' Jessica admitted. 'I came to see the Dales. Which parts would you particularly recommend?'

His eyes had dropped to the book still open in front of her at the photograph of Morley, a faint compression appearing momentarily about his mouth. 'If you're interested in old houses you couldn't do better than visit that place—early eighteeenth century, and beautifully preserved. It's open today.'

'So I see.' She kept her tone carefully neutral. 'I might do that. It isn't too far from here, is it?'

'About fifteen miles. You take the Skipton road and turn right at the sign for Morley. The Grange is out the far side of the village. You can't go wrong.'

'Thanks.' Jessica closed the book and gathered it up as the waitress came across to take Peter's order, smilingly shaking her head in answer to his look of enquiry. 'I really have had enough, but I enjoyed the company.'

'What about tonight?' he asked swiftly before she could rise. 'Do you plan on staying over?'

'Yes,' she admitted. 'I'm booked in till Monday morning.'

'In that case, let me pick you up around seven and

take you out to supper. There's no evening surgery Saturdays.' He saw the hesitation in the green eyes and gave a small, deprecatory shrug. 'Better than spending the whole evening alone.'

Jessica made up her mind quickly. What harm would it do? 'Very much better,' she agreed. 'Thanks, I'd like that. Enjoy your breakfast.'

Her Mini was parked round the back of the hotel in the space allocated. If she left now, she calculated, she would reach Morley around ten-thirty, which was when the Grange opened for visiting parties. If she got it over with she might feel able to settle to the rest of her holiday with an easier mind. Certainly she would not be concentrating on a great deal else until she had satisfied that gnawing need to know.

As Peter had said, the route was not difficult to follow. Once off the main road she found herself in countryside so sparsely populated she met only one other vehicle in three miles of driving, and that a tractor. There was a rugged grandeur about the lofting hillsides, a fascination in the endlessly varying patterns created by the drystone walls bisecting the land in every direction. Occasionally she passed a farmhouse standing in splendid isolation, but with little sign of activity anywhere. All hands must be busy in barns or hidden by undulations in the landscape, she surmised. Certainly there had to be someone to look after the sheep and cattle grazing in the odd field.

She came on the village quite suddenly, topping a rise to coast down a steepish hill and over a humpback bridge into the single main street flanked by grey stone cottages and a couple of shops. There was a pub too, she noted in passing—the Plough; not very original, but it suited the setting. There were people on the street, even a car or two parked at the kerbside. One of the latter pulled out and fell into line behind her as she headed out of the village and up the hill on the far side of the little valley. Perhaps someone else looking for the Grange too—she hoped so. She had counted on mingling with a reasonable group of people for her tour of her grandmother's former home.

The car stayed behind her, though at a safe enough distance, when she followed the signpost at the crossroads. She could see the house for several minutes before she reached the big double entrance gates to the estate and had an uninterrupted view of it while driving the half-mile length of the curving drive. It was beautifully proportioned, its two main façades flanking a central bay, with little surface decoration to mar its graceful lines. The white sash windows caught the morning sunlight, creating an air of warmth and welcome which pulled at Jessica's heartstrings.

The drive terminated in a sweeping circle about a huge central flower bed in front of the main doors, but before that a section signposted 'Parking' branched off around the side of the house and through a stone archway to finish up in the yard of what Jessica took to be stable buildings, although there were no horses in sight. Her own, and an estate car now pulling into the yard behind her, were the only vehicles in evidence too. So much for anonymity, she thought wryly, seeing only one person in the other car. Two people hardly constituted a group. It was even possible that it wouldn't be considered worthwhile taking them round, considering.

Switching off the engine, she got out of the car to stand looking across at the house, contemplating a change of mind about proceeding any farther. She had seen the place, which was all she had really wanted. Why not settle for that?

'You're an early bird,' commented the driver of the other car cheerfully, coming over. 'We don't normally get anyone before the afternoon. You are here to see the place, I take it?'

'I was,' she acknowledged, looking round at him with suddenly faster beating heart. 'You live here?'

'Leo Stafford, at your service, ma'am,' he came back with exaggerated olde-worlde courtesy. His eyes had a wicked sparkle. 'The black sheep of the family, according to my elders and betters. If it's a tour you're looking for I can give you the whole works from an inside position, so to speak.'

A rebel, Jessica decided, unable to keep the smile from her lips. A chip off the same block as her grandmother, perhaps. Too handsome for his own good, she could almost hear those self-same elders and betters saying. The dark hair and vivid blue eyes were enough in themselves to set most female pulses racing. If her own was proving the exception that was most likely because she knew herself related, even if distantly. He looked about her own age, which probably made him a third cousin. Hardly worth considering, yet it was there. Grandmother's great-nephew, he would have been.

'Perhaps I should come back this afternoon,' she murmured, 'then I can have the regular tour.'

'Ah, but that would cost you a pound, and this one's free,' he countered. 'You can't turn down an offer like that. It's bad for my ego, for one thing.'

Jessica laughed, suddenly giving way. What difference did it make in the long run? No one knew who she was. 'I'll come,' she said, 'but on one condition—you have to let me pay my pound. After all, maintenance on a place this size must be astronomical, and every little helps.'

'Right on both counts,' he agreed. 'All right, a pound it is, and I'll endeavour to give you full value for money. We'll start with the main hall, only it saves time and effort if we go in the back way. You don't mind using the tradesmen's entrance, do you?'

'Not at all.' His charm was impossible to resist. 'You lead and I'll follow.'

'We'll walk together,' he said, taking her arm companionably. 'Like civilised human beings. Now let's see—the house was built around 1720 by one of my illustrious ancestors, a certain Charles Stafford, a bit of a rake, by all accounts. He's said to have fathered a whole passel of illegitimate children. Luckily he had some born the right side of the blanket too, or lord only knows what would have happened to the blood line!'

'Let's stick to the normal detail, shall we?' suggested Jessica dryly. 'Historical rather than histrionic.'

His grin was unabashed. 'Dull but safe, I suppose. This door here, then we give the kitchens a miss. Our present cook gets temperamental when it comes to visitors getting under her feet, and cooks are difficult enough to find these days, much less to keep.'

The passage in which they found themselves was stone-flagged and cool after the warmth of the June sun. Doors opened off it to either side, but Leo kept right on going, turning corners until they eventually emerged into a large pillared hall under the curve of the staircase. A two-flighted grand staircase, Jessica realised as they moved farther into the room, the division taking place only six stairs up at the first landing. The right-hand flight was roped off, with a small sign saying 'Private' attached to the rope. Portraits lined the white plastered walls.

'Ancestors,' Leo advised, following the direction of her gaze. 'The South Wing is purely family—plus friends of family, of course. Even in winter we don't use the whole house. All told, there are twenty-seven rooms. Why anybody should have needed a place that large defies imagination!'

'Status symbol?' Jessica suggested. 'A lot of store was surely set by appearances. At least it was designed with taste and discretion—the proportions are perfect.'

'Are you in architecture?' he asked with some interest, and she smiled, shaking her head.

'Just a common or garden secretary taking a holiday.'

'Don't knock your own talents. Good secretaries are few and far between.'

She glanced at him sideways. 'What makes you so sure I'm good at my job?'

'Instinct,' he said. 'And I'm rarely wrong about people. Do you want to start downstairs or up?'

'Down,' she decided. 'The views from upstairs must be magnificent—I'd like to save them till last.'

Despite the fact that only one half of the house was on public view, the tour of the lower floor alone took more than thirty minutes. The rooms were beautifully kept, the décor a restrained mingling of eighteenth and early nineteenth century with lots of white plasterwork picked out in gilt. No tatty, cast-out antiquity here. Each piece of furniture had obviously been chosen with care to fit a certain spot, the woods and fabrics maintained in pristine condition. It seemed a shame, Jessica thought, that no one used such lovely settings, yet if there were as many rooms as these in the other wing she could well see why.

Upstairs was no exception, the bedrooms elegant with their fourposters and silk-swathed windows. The rear of the house looked out over formal gardens and a small lake to the high moors. Along the greater part of the east front ran a magnificent Long Gallery, its ceiling elaborately decorated in plaster. At one time it had been three interconnecting rooms, Leo had told her, until someone had hit on the idea of knocking through the inner walls to form this one superb vista. The carpet which stretched the full length had been specially made to come apart in sections so that it could be taken up for dancing on occasion.

'It's become a tradition that Morley holds a Grand Ball every July,' he added on a note of irony. 'Another status symbol, perhaps. It's the only time when all the bedrooms are in full use—including those in the North Wing.'

'It must cost a fortune,' Jessica commented practically, trying to imagine the detail involved. 'To say nothing of just keeping the place up to the standard set. I shouldn't have thought the odd pound or two from visiting tourists would even scratch the surface.'

'It doesn't.' Leo was smiling. 'You know, it isn't often we get someone along who even stops to think about the cost of maintenance. All they usually do is grumble that a pound is far too much. Considering the damage caused by the number of feet that pass through the place during open season, I'd say they get off pretty lightly.'

'Why do it at all if it doesn't pay?' Jessica asked curiously, and saw his shoulders lift in a shrug.

'Because Craig happens to believe we owe the public a look at their own heritage. Owners, in his view, are simply custodians, here to preserve history.'

'Craig?'

'My older brother—master of the house.' The last with faint satire. 'Not that he's very often in it. His business interests lie elsewhere.'

Another cousin, thought Jessica, and knew a sudden temptation to tell Leo the truth. This was her family too, the only family she had left. She wanted nothing from them except recognition.

'Something troubling you?' Leo was looking at her curiously. 'You've gone very serious.'

She forced a smile, the moment for confidences past. 'I was just thinking about something. If you're not the usual guide, who would normally be taking the tour?'

'Oh, we have an official potted-history man, complete with uniform. He sits out in the outer hall waiting for customers.'

'I didn't see that.'

'You weren't intended to. I might have got across

some demarcation line.' They had reached the head of the staircase again. He added swiftly, 'How about some coffee before you go? On the house this time.'

'What about your family?' she countered. 'Won't they object to you bringing in a paying customer for free drinks?'

'Craig is in Harrogate, Mother usually stays in her own rooms until lunchtime weekends and Great-Uncle Philip is confined to bed with a chill,' he pronounced with an air of settling matters. 'Not that it makes any difference. So far as anyone else is concerned, you're here as a friend.'

Jessica gave in without a struggle, wanting to prolong her departure as much as Leo apparently did. 'In that case, yes, I would like some coffee.'

The sitting room to which he took her was just as finely furnished and cared for as its counterpart on the other side of the house, but with a lived-in atmosphere the other rooms had lacked. Magazines and a couple of books lay on the mahogany coffee table, while someone's knitting had been left tucked into a corner of the brocade sofa.

'My mother's,' Leo acknowledged, seeing her glance. 'The maid knows better than to touch it.'

'A bit of a martinet, is she?' Jessica asked casually as he went over to tug on a brocade bell pull at the side of the Adam fireplace.

'Who, Mother?' He laughed and shook his head. 'Only when it comes to her knitting. She likes to find it right where she left it. Do you knit?'

'I've never tried,' Jessica confessed.

'Good for you. I've never seen Mother finish anything, if it comes to that. I think it's more of an occupational therapy.' He looked round as the door opened to admit a young woman in a plain dark dress. 'Bring some coffee, will you, Pauline.'

The girl nodded by way of acknowledgement, gave

Jessica a speculative once-over and departed the way she had come, leaving the door ajar. Sighing, Leo went to close it.

'You see what I mean about staff these days? No idea at all.'

'Different attitudes,' Jessica commented without particular inflection. 'Do you carry a lot of staff?'

'Nowhere near enough for the size of the place—two maids, the cook, an odd-job man and a team of daily domestics. Oh, then there's the gardeners, of course. Three of those. And the gamekeeper. The estate runs to a great many acres.' He came over to take a seat beside her on the sofa, stretching his legs comfortably in front of him. 'There'll be a butler again when we find the right man. The last one retired three months ago after forty years, and he's going to take some replacing. The same with the estate office secretary. She has to leave in a hurry because her mother had an accident and needs care and attention, which leaves us with less than a week to find a replacement. Pity you're only here on holiday, you'd fill the bill nicely.'

Jessica's heart had done a double beat, now it seemed to lift into her throat. 'You don't even know what qualifications I hold,' she heard herself saying, as if from a distance.

'Whatever, I'm pretty sure they'd be more than adequate. No one who talks and acts the way you do could be less than competent.' He paused suddenly, looking at her with a changed expression. 'I say, you wouldn't consider it, would you? It would be a godsend not to have to start advertising. You wouldn't lose on it, by any means. We'd top whatever salary you're getting now.' He stopped again, face falling a little. 'I'm getting ahead of myself. You're hardly going to be able to get out of your present job without notice.'

'As a matter of fact ...' her voice sounded odd ... 'I'm between jobs right now. I left my last one because I needed a change, and so far I haven't done anything about finding another.'

'But that makes things perfect!' Leo was leaning towards her, blue eyes alight with enthusiasm. 'You'd be ideal.' He laughed. 'You know, I don't even know your name yet.'

She told him, trying not to let her emotions take over from common sense. If she took a job here she would be doing so under false pretences, condemning herself to carrying a secret she would never dare to reveal. Yet if she turned this offer down, what then? A return to London and the life she had fled? The thought held little appeal. Here in Yorkshire she would be with her own relatives, even if they never knew it; a member of the Stafford household for as long as she could keep up the masquerade. The temptation was overwhelming.

'Would I be working for you?' she asked, playing for time.

'You'd be working for the estate,' he said. 'Bob Grainger manages it, along with my help.' The last with a quirk of his lips which made light of the statement. 'He's getting on, and harassed enough without having to think about hiring and firing. He'd bless my soul for having found you.' His tone softened, deliberately coaxing. 'I have found you, haven't I?'

'It sounds the kind of thing I'm looking for,' she agreed weakly. 'What about references? I don't have them with me, I'm afraid.'

'You can bring them when you come, just for the look of the thing, but I don't need references to tell me you're honest and worthy and all that claptrap. I'll take responsibility if you do turn out to be after the silver.' The sparkle was in his eyes again. 'Actually, I do have another personal reason for wanting you to take the job. Miss Branston is a real spinster type, chosen by my brother who didn't have to work with her. Both Bob and I deserve an improvement in the office scenery.

How long would it take you to organise yourself?'

Jessica had the feeling that fate was carrying her deeper and deeper into this. Why fight it? she thought. 'If I leave after lunch I can be back in London this evening,' she said. 'Say next Wednesday.'

'That would fit in just right. Miss Branston leaves Friday. She'd be able to show you the ropes before she went. What about your holiday, though?'

Right now that was the least of her considerations. She shook her head. 'If I'm going to be living here I'll see all I would have seen, and more. There'd be the usual month's trial either side, I imagine?'

'Well, from our point of view I hardly think it necessary, but I suppose there's always the chance you might not be able to take the rural scene.' For the first time an element of doubt entered Leo's expression. 'Harrogate is the nearest town, and that can hardly offer the brand of night life you must be accustomed to.'

'It's a fallacy,' she told him, 'that people who live in or close to London spend every night living it up in the West End. Few I know could afford it, for one thing, and for another, I'm personally not very interested in laid-on entertainment of that kind. Some of my best evenings have been spent listening to band concerts in the park.'

'You've never been to the right places,' Leo returned. 'I spent most weekends in the city when I was at Cambridge, and had a ball! I'd sell my soul to be back there right now.'

'Then why don't you?' Jessica asked curiously. 'Go, I mean.'

His smile had a wry tilt. 'Doing what? My income isn't enough to keep me in any style without a job to supplement it, and I'm hardly qualified for anything at the level I'd want, according to Craig.'

Big Brother again. Jessica was beginning to dislike

the man even before she had met him. 'What about if and when you marry? Your wife may not want to stay in Yorkshire.'

Just for a moment there was a bleak look in his eyes. 'I'll have to cross that bridge if and when I come to it.'

Their coffee arrived with a bang as the door flew open to Pauline's push. Looking totally unperturbed, she came over to deposit the tray she carried on the sofa table, knocking a magazine to the floor in doing so.

'Cook says if there's going to be an extra for lunch she'd like to know,' she announced.

'Thanks, but no,' Jessica said hurriedly as Leo lifted enquiring brows in her direction. 'I'll have it at the hotel before I leave.'

'Right, I'll tell her,' acknowledged the girl.

Leo watched her leave with a despairing expression. 'Lawson would have thrown several fits if he'd heard that! If we can't find another butler it will have to be a housekeeper—anyone who can get this house to run smoothly again. Pity you can't stay on to lunch,' he added, turning back. 'You could have met Mother.'

'What about the estate manager himself?' Jessica asked. 'Shouldn't I at least be vetted?'

'He isn't here today.' A stubborn look crossed the handsome features. 'Anyway, Bob would be the first to agree about taking advantage of opportunity while it exists. He'll be highly relieved to have found a replacement so quickly. My typing is strictly the two-fingered variety. Don't worry, everyone will be in the picture by the time you get back. Miss Branston lives out, but you'll be living in, of course. Try and make it in time for dinner, then you can meet the whole family.'

'I'll be here by teatime,' Jessica promised. She drank the last of her coffee and got to her feet, her mind still a little dazed from the speed at which it had all happened. 'Till Wednesday then, Mr Stafford.'

'Hey!' His tone was chiding. 'The name's Leo. The

only Mr Stafford round here is my brother.'

'A lot older than you, is he?' she speculated as they moved towards the door.

'Only ten years, though you'd never believe it. I suppose being left the head of the family at twenty-three had a lot to do with it. What about your family?' he added as an afterthought. 'Do you still live at home?'

'My parents are both dead,' Jessica said unemotionally. 'At present I share a flat with another girl, but she won't have any trouble finding someone else to share. Her boy-friend is practically a fixture now.'

'Their gain is ours too.' They had passed through the archway into the main hall. Now Leo inclined his head towards a portrait on the near wall. 'This is Craig. It's traditional to have the present master of Morley hung here. On his death he'll be relegated to the staircase, with all the others moved up a space to accommodate him.'

Jessica would have liked time in which to study the painting thoroughly. As it was she was left only a fleeting impression of lean, unsmiling features and eyes like chips of grey steel. Certainly there was little, if any, resemblance to the young man at her side.

'I take after my mother's side of the family, while Craig inherited the Stafford looks and colouring,' Leo advised, moving on. 'We're quite different types. He's due to leave on an overseas trip anytime, so you may not meet him for several weeks.' His tone suggested she might count herself fortunate in that. 'We'll go out the back way again, it's closer.'

Another couple of vehicles were already parked close by Jessica's car when they got outside, the occupants not in evidence.

'George must be taking them round,' said Leo, opening her door for her to get behind the wheel. 'There should be others along soon.' His tone altered. 'You won't let me down, will you, Jessica?'

'Of course not.' The casual way in which she had been hired still bothered her to a certain extent, but she wasn't going to let that put her off now. 'I'll be back Wednesday afternoon without fail.' She held out her hand. 'Thanks again.'

She could see him looking after her as she drove off, then she had turned the corner of the house and he was gone. The sun lay directly overhead in a cloudless blue sky, shimmering the long white drive ahead in heat. A big silver-grey Mercedes turned in at the gates as she approached, coming towards her too fast and with an air of owning right of way that caused Jessica to pull instinctively to the extreme edge of the drive.

She saw the driver for bare seconds in passing, but it was long enough to recognise the uncompromising set of his features. Craig Stafford—master of Morley. She had a sudden premonition that this was only the first of many times in which she was to come up against her elder cousin.

CHAPTER TWO

THERE were times during the following hectic few days when doubt almost gained the upper hand. She was being a fool, Jessica acknowledged on such occasions. To take a job for reasons such as hers was bad enough in itself, to do so on as casual a footing infinitely worse. Charming her cousin Leo might be, businesslike he was not. For all she knew he might not even have the authority to hire a replacement for Miss Branston without his brother's approval. Certainly he had given the impression that Craig Stafford ruled the roost where Morley was concerned.

The obvious solution, of course, was to telephone the house and verify her position, yet something in her shrank from that particular course of action. As long as her whereabouts was unknown she could not be informed of any change in circumstances, and once there at Morley she would surely be entitled to the benefit of a fair trial at least. Craig was to be away by the time she arrived, according to what Leo had told her. By the time he returned she would have proved her worth; she would make sure of that.

Her future plans she left deliberately vague. Perhaps one day, when she felt she knew the family well enough, she would reveal her relationship—or then again, perhaps not. The important thing was in having found them at all. She no longer felt alone.

Owing to one thing and another, it was later than she had intended when she finally left the Bayswater flat on the Wednesday, and the pre-noon traffic was already building up. Jessica stopped for lunch before getting on to the M1 and made good time on that first leg of her journey north. Nevertheless, it was almost five-thirty by the time she had threaded her way around the outskirts of Leeds and found the Ilkley road.

The engine failure which occurred some twenty minutes later was a classic, in that it happened on a stretch of road seemingly miles from anywhere, and with little in the way of passing traffic to provide assistance. Her scanty knowledge of possible mechanical faults exhausted, Jessica was only too glad to accept a lift to the nearest village from the elderly lady driver who eventually happened along, thankful to find the local garage still open for business.

The mechanic who took her back to the scene of the breakdown was young and cheerful and in no particular hurry to get things done. 'Have to take it in,' he announced after a couple of futile attempts to start the engine and a somewhat cursory glance under the bonnet. 'Could be anything.'

For Jessica that was the start of two long and frustrating hours while she waited for the trouble to be located and rectified. She spent the greater part of the time in the tiny café opposite the garage eating a meal of sausage, chips and egg and drinking innumerable cups of tea while cursing the luck which had caused this to happen today of all days. She should, she knew, telephone the house to let them know she would be late, yet the same reservations held her hand. Supposing they told her not to come—that Leo had been wrong in offering her the job. It was too late to start turning back. She had to go on, come what may.

Dusk was creeping across the fields by the time the Mini was ready. She paid the bill by credit card, adding a tip in cash for the mechanic who had stayed on after hours to help her out. From here to Morley was approximately thirty miles, she reckoned. If she put her foot down she could still be there before nine. Hardly an auspicious start, but it couldn't be helped.

Her watch said eight-fifty when she finally turned in through the big double gates, luckily left open. The house was well lit, its bulk as gracious as she remembered it even by night. A couple of cars were parked at an angle on the wide gravel apron in front of the house. Jessica put the Mini in beside a long red Ferrari she was almost sure would belong to Leo, and took her overnight case from the boot with a firming of resolve. No matter what happened now, she was here and she was staying.

It seemed to take a long time for the doorbell to be answered. She was on the point of ringing again when the door was finally opened by a maid dressed neatly and traditionally in black and white.

'I'm Jessica Chappel,' Jessica announced in what she hoped were suitably confident tones. 'I believe I'm expected.'

Older than the girl she had seen on her previous visit by a good twenty years, and certainly more experienced at her job, the maid nevertheless revealed a look of disconcertion.

'They'd given you up,' she said. 'They thought you weren't coming after all.'

Hoped might be closer the mark, Jessica surmised wryly from the tone of that statement, and steeled herself against the sudden urge to cut and run.

'My car broke down,' she said by way of explanation. 'Perhaps you'd fetch Mr Stafford himself.'

'Yes, of course.' Recovering, the woman opened the door wider. 'You'd better come in, miss.'

Jessica did so, passing through the narrow outer hall to the well-remembered inner, lit now by a glowing central chandelier and several wall brackets. Despite its size and antiquity the house felt lived-in, warm and welcoming. Once her grandmother had trod these same polished floor tiles, mounted those wide balustraded stairs now closely carpeted in muted red. Little would have altered from those days. A place like this was timeless.

'They've just finished dinner,' advised the maid, casting a glance at the overnight bag in Jessica's hand. 'Perhaps you'd like to sit down while I tell Mr Stafford you're here.'

At least she wasn't interrupting the meal, Jessica thought thankfully. That was something. She took a curved and padded chair by the wall, hoping Leo would come alone; she wasn't yet ready to meet any other member of the family.

The portrait opposite drew her eyes like a magnet. It was almost as if it watched her. On impulse she got up again and went over to study it at closer quarters, taking in the sardonic quality about the mouth, the tautness of skin over hard-boned features. An attractive face, she acknowledged, if one liked total masculinity in a man. There was no element of softness about it.

A door opened on the far side of the hall, emitting the sound of voices along with the uniformed figure of the maid. The latter avoided Jessica's eyes as she came across.

'If you'd like to wait in the study, Mr Stafford will be along in a moment,' she said. 'This way.'

Jessica followed her, wryly aware of being put in her place. It didn't seem like the man she had met a few days ago, yet what did she really know of him? She should have phoned to let him know she was on her way. Leaving him in the air like this had been thoughtless, to say the least. If he was feeling a little put out she could hardly blame him too much.

The study was down one of the corridors, a comfortable, booklined room containing a chesterfield and easy chairs in addition to the expected desk and other accoutrements. Left alone, Jessica advanced to take a seat in one of the deep club chairs, looking about her as she did so. Essentially a man's room, she thought, viewing the hunting prints on the walls, the preponderance of leather, the titles of the books close enough to be read. Not exactly the kind of room she would have associated with Leo Stafford, but he no doubt had little to say in the general décor. As the younger son he was simply a hanger-on, living in a house that would almost certainly never be his. One could sympathise with that kind of deprivation.

Footsteps sounded along the corridor outside. Smiling, and with an apology ready on her lips, she turned towards the door as it opened, face stiffening involuntarily on sight of the newcomer. Craig Stafford was both taller and broader in the shoulder than his brother, a leanly built, powerful-looking man with the same steely glint about the eyes that she had noted in the portrait. He was wearing a dark suede jacket over a rollnecked white sweater which emphasised the tan of his skin. The light from the nearby wall bracket picked up a hint of red in the thick dark brown of his hair.

'I don't think this need take long,' he said without preamble. 'Naturally you'll be reimbursed for your trouble, but I'm afraid you had a wasted journey.' Having barely glanced at her, he was already moving towards the mahogany desk, covering the ground with a few purposeful strides to open a drawer and take out what looked like a cheque book. 'The pub in the village will put you up for the night if you'd prefer a clear run back to London in the morning,' he added, picking up a pen from the silver tray at the rear of the desk. 'You can tell them to send the bill up here.'

Jessica came slowly to her feet, surprised by her own steadiness. 'I think we'd better start again, Mr Stafford,' she said.

This time he did look at her, a long, measuring look which took in every detail of her slim, shapely figure in the neat green suit before coming back to her face. There was no change of expression to be seen about the lean features; certainly there was no softening of the grey eyes.

'There isn't much point in discussing matters.'

'There's every point,' she came back. 'Your brother offered me a job which I accepted. That, so far as I'm concerned, gives me certain rights.'

'A casual arrangement made over a cup of coffee gives you precisely nothing.' The statement was brusque. 'Did you really imagine you'd just walk in here and take over the job on the strength of one man's weakness for a pretty face?'

'I have qualifications,' she insisted, determined not to let him get to her. 'My references are right here in my purse if you'd like to see them.'

'Thanks, but no.' He wasn't giving an inch. 'The whole situation is quite unsatisfactory. We know nothing about you. You could be anybody.'

I'm your cousin, she was strongly tempted to say, but this was neither the time nor place. 'I can fill in any details you need to know,' she said instead, 'and my former employers will vouch for my honesty. I gave up my London flat to come here, and finding another won't be easy. Mistake or not, I think you owe me the courtesy of a fair trial.'

One dark brow lifted faintly. 'Do you indeed? And how long a trial would you consider fair?'

'A month either side is the norm.' Jessica returned his gaze without flinching, the irony just discernible in her voice. 'After all, I might not like the job myself.'

'Oh quite.' He studied her for another moment or two, expression hard to define. When he moved it was abruptly, holding out a hand. 'Give me your references and sit down.'

Jessica obeyed both injunctions, taking an upright chair on her own side of the desk with a feeling that while not yet out of the wood she was beginning to win through. Craig sat down too, switching on the desk lamp as he did so. She watched him as he read the letter she had given him, comparing the living features in front of her with the portrait in her mind's eye. A good likeness, she had to admit. The artist had captured the essence of the man with remarkable clarity. Nothing about Craig Stafford suggested weakness of any kind, yet everyone had their Achilles heel. It would be interesting to speculate on what his might be.

'Very impressive,' he said at length, folding the letter back along its original lines. 'Tell me, why did you leave your last job?'

'I needed a change,' she admitted. 'I was getting stale.'

'But why choose Yorkshire to look for it? Why not closer to home?'

Her shrug was as casual as she could make it. 'If I was going to have a change at all it seemed as well to make it a total one. As it happens, I wasn't actually looking for a job when I met your brother, I was taking a touring holiday.'

'So I gathered.' His gaze didn't waver. 'Running away from something?'

Despite herself she stiffened. 'Would that really be any of your concern?'

'It would depend,' he returned evenly, 'on what it was you were running away from. A man, perhaps?' His mouth tilted faintly at the fleeting change of expression in her eyes. 'That appears to have hit a tender spot. Did he find himself another girl?'

'If you like.' She saw no reason to involve herself in further explanations. Let him think what he wanted to think. 'Can we leave my private life out of it, please?'

'It explains the aggression,' he said as if she hadn't spoken. 'One let-down and the whole male sex becomes a target for resentment.'

'Hardly all,' Jessica retorted softly. 'I found your brother charming.'

'I'm sure you did.' If the innuendo had registered he wasn't revealing it. 'Leo could, as we say in these parts, charm the ducks right out of the water.' The pause was brief. 'What exactly did he tell you about the job?'

'Not a lot.' She hated to admit it but saw no way of bluffing her way through that one. 'Just that I'd be working for the estate office in place of a Miss Branston who's leaving. He did say she'd be here until Friday.'

'Yes, she will. Whether you'll be staying yourself is still open to doubt.'

'Why?' she demanded, throwing caution aside. 'You're satisfied with my references—you just said so. What *else* do I have to do to impress you, Mr Stafford?'

'You could try putting a curb on your temper by way of a start,' he returned without raising his voice. 'I have one of my own.'

Jessica bit her lip, aware that she deserved the rebuke. 'I'm sorry,' she offered, low-toned. 'I think I must be tired.'

'Hardly surprising if you've been travelling all day.' He was silent for a long moment looking at her, a frown creasing the space between his brows. When he did speak it was decisively. 'I'll be straight with you—I don't care for the way this was arranged, and I'm still not at all sure you're the right person for this job, but having said that I'm willing to give you the benefit of the doubt for the next month.' He stayed her reply with a lifted hand. 'No, hear me out. One thing I want making clear. There's to be no relationship of any kind between you and my brother outside of the job itself. Understood?'

Had it not been for certain pressing personal reasons, Jessica would have told him there and then what he could do with his precious job, but he was only one member of this family. Her nod was perfunctory. 'Perfectly.'

'Good.' He came to his feet, replacing the cheque

book in the drawer from which he had taken it. 'I'll have someone show you your room.'

'You mean you have one already prepared?' She could not resist the dig. 'That's what I call covering all eventualities!'

'My brother's orders, not mine,' came the unmoved reply. 'I was only told you were expected this morning when he realised my overseas trip had been postponed.'

'So naturally you insisted on vetting me yourself.'

'Naturally.' One lean finger rested briefly on the bellpush set into the desk top. 'As I said, Leo's judgment isn't always reliable. You have to admit the situation is hardly orthodox. You're staying purely on the strength of your references, not because I feel in any way obliged to take you on. Incidentally, I take it you've no objections to my checking with your previous employers?'

There was only one reply she could make to that. 'None at all.'

He looked away from her as the door opened again. 'Show Miss Chappel to her room, will you, Pauline.' To Jessica he added, 'What about your bags?'

'They're out in the car,' she said. 'Apart from a small overnight case I left in the hall.'

'Leave your keys and they'll be brought up to you. Have you eaten?'

She nodded. 'I had a meal while I was waiting for my car to be fixed. I broke down about thirty miles from here.'

'So I understood.' Tone dry, he added, 'An early night should help you recover from the stresses and strains. Breakfast is at eight-thirty, except for weekends when it's flexible. Goodnight, Miss Chappel.'

Jessica made her escape from the room with relief, aware of antagonism bristling inside her. The man was a despot, there was no doubt about that. Morley only had one master, and he was making sure she realised it.

She smarted for Leo, so summarily dismissed.

'So you're staying after all,' commented Pauline out in the corridor. Her curiosity was patent. 'Never thought he'd let you after what he said to Mr Leo this morning. Called him an irresponsible idiot!'

'In front of you?' Jessica queried with lifted brows.

'Well, no, not really.' The admittance was made without shame. 'I just happened to be passing the library when they were in there, that's all. Mr Leo was real upset, only Mr Stafford didn't care. He said there was no way Mr Leo was going to install one of his passing fancies in the house.' The last with a certain relish. 'Mr Leo said . . .'

'I don't really want to hear what Mr Leo said.' Jessica kept her tone level. 'And you shouldn't have listened either.'

'I didn't have to listen. You could have heard them from across the hall.' Pauline sounded sulky and more than a little resentful. 'Always going on at him about something, he is. Everybody knows that!'

'I've just arrived,' Jessica pointed out. 'And I'd prefer to form my own opinions.' She softened the words with a smile. 'Have you been here long yourself?'

'Six months,' the girl replied, leading the way upstairs. 'I wouldn't stay, only it's handy for home. I live in the village, you see. Mum used to work here when she was a girl, though they had a lot more staff here then. I was going to leave anyway if Lawson hadn't retired. A real old bat, he was!'

Lawson, Jessica remembered, was the former butler. 'Who runs the house now?' she asked.

'Oh, Mrs Stafford does it herself. She's all right.'

Leo took after his mother's side of the family, Jessica recalled. She had to be all right. Craig was another matter entirely—the autocratic elder son who had inherited more than his fair share of everything. No relationship with my brother, he had said, but that surely didn't include common friendship. Leo needed all the friends he could get, by all accounts.

Her room was at the rear of the house overlooking the moonlit lake. It was large and airy, with its own adjoining bathroom and a small private balcony. Draped in turquoise silk to match the curtains at the long, Georgian windows, the bed looked inviting, bringing home to Jessica just how weary she really was. The early night was a good idea—she had to agree with that. It gave her time to collect herself in readiness for the morning when she would meet the rest of the Stafford family.

A middle-aged man in shirt-sleeves brought up her luggage some minutes later. Taciturn to the point of almost total non-communication, he simply grunted an acknowledgement when Jessica thanked him, and left. It took her less than half an hour to unpack her things, and a mere ten minutes to take a bath and get into her nightclothes. By half past ten she was in bed with the lights out watching the moon shadows on the wall by the nearest window. The people who lived in this house were her closest kin, and she was now one of them. What happened from now on remained to be seen.

She was awake at seven, refreshed from a sleep undisturbed by even a dream that she could recall. The view from her balcony was superb, the air fresh and scented the way only an English June morning could smell. A horse and rider could be seen cantering across a distant field, pace lengthening even as she watched to take the hedge at the far side. Leo or Craig? From this distance she couldn't be sure. Whichever, the man could certainly ride.

Another horse was approaching now from the opposite direction. Jessica saw the two of them come together and halt, the riders apparently falling into discussion. Instinct told her the newcomer was a woman, although it could equally well be a smaller man, she supposed. It was a perfect morning for a ride. Jessica envied the ability she had never herself acquired. Perhaps she could learn while she was here.

Dressed in tailored grey cotton, she made her way downstairs a little before the half hour, pausing irresolutely in the hall to study the various closed doors. One of them had to be the dining room, but which? Or maybe there was a breakfast room. She would feel a fool searching every one for signs of occupation.

Footsteps sounded on the stairs behind her, and she turned to see Leo smiling at her with every sign of genuine pleasure.

'Jessica! Glad you made it. I knew you wouldn't let me down.'

'I hate letting people down,' she said. 'I should have phoned through to clarify matters long before this.'

'If you had you'd probably have got Craig anyway, and he'd have scotched the whole idea.' His tone was wry. 'Sorry to put you through all that last night, but he insisted on seeing you himself. To tell you the truth, I didn't expect you to be here at all this morning.'

'You mean you didn't think your brother would allow me to stay.' Her smile was reminiscent. 'Let's just say I managed to convince him I had a little more to my credit than he seemed to believe. I'm on a month's trial.'

'So are we, I gather.' Leo was laughing, blue eyes appreciative. 'I hope you can put up with us—Craig included.'

'I'll do my best,' she promised, feeling rather more confident by the light of day. 'I was told breakfast was eight-thirty sharp.'

'So it is. They're probably out there already.' He took her lightly by the arm, moving her in the direction of the same corridor she had traversed the night before. 'We'll make the grand entrance together.'

The breakfast room was at the rear of the house too, opening directly on to the stone-flagged terrace. They were eating outside, Jessica found to her delight. On a morning like this there could be nothing better.

Craig was already seated at the head of the cloth-covered table, a newspaper held in front of him. He lowered it on their approach, revealing another of the silky sweaters, this time in pale beige. The grey eyes regarded the two of them with cynicism.

'Good morning,' he said. 'I hope you slept well.'

'Very well, thanks,' Jessica answered. 'It's a beautiful morning!'

'Isn't it,' he agreed dryly. 'Mother, meet Jessica Chappel. She's going to be staying with us for a time.'

'A long time, I hope,' said the greying but still attractive woman seated at the other end of the table. Her smile was a replica of her younger son's. 'Come and sit here by me and tell me about yourself. You're different from what I imagined.'

'What she means,' put in Leo suavely, taking the chair opposite Jessica's, 'is that you're different from the kind of girls I usually show an interest in. Horses for courses, sweetheart. Jessica is another proposition.'

'That's right.' Jessica said it before Craig could. 'I'm here to work.'

'But not all of the time,' Mrs Stafford rejoined on a light note. 'It's going to be nice having someone to talk to in the evenings apart from these sons of mine—especially while my daughter is still away. Not that Beth is much of a companion at the best of times.' The fond note in her voice took any sting out of the words. 'I suppose at twenty I felt I had better things to do than chat with Mummy too.'

'It's time she got back,' said her elder son without lowering the newspaper. 'She'll have forgotten what home looks like before long.'

'Well, you were the one who suggested this trip,'

returned Mrs Stafford mildly. 'Why don't you tell her to come on home?' She turned back to Jessica without waiting for any reply, pushing across the silver pot in front of her. 'Help yourself to coffee—or would you prefer tea?'

'Coffee will be fine,' Jessica assured her. She took it black, sipping gratefully at the hot, aromatic liquid. 'I shall only need toast to go with this. I don't normally eat much breakfast.'

'Then it's about time you did,' put in Craig, coming out from behind the newspaper as the elder of the two maids emerged from the house with a loaded tray. 'You can't work on an empty stomach.'

'Perhaps *you* can't,' she countered smoothly without turning her head, 'but that's another matter. We're all individuals, Mr Stafford.'

'And that puts you in your place!' His mother was laughing. 'Leave the girl alone, Craig. She's only just got here.'

Green eyes met grey and flickered away again, unable to withstand the directness of his regard. 'I'm sorry if that sounded rude,' Jessica apologised. 'It wasn't meant to be.'

'No offence taken,' he said. 'You're entitled to ruin your health any way you want to. Would you like to pass the coffee down here?'

Jessica did so, conscious of derision in the line of his mouth. She hadn't meant to apologise; the words had been dragged from her. She had a feeling he was well accustomed to putting people at a disadvantage that way.

'If you're taking a few days off,' said Mrs Stafford into the small silence, 'you might consider spending an hour or two running me into Harrogate either today or tomorrow. I hate driving alone. I have to see Breams about my dress for the Ball. I showed them the style I wanted in Harrod's catalogue, but I think I might change my mind.'

'You only have two weeks,' he rejoined. 'Do you have time to change your mind?'

'I'd better—and stop trying to avoid the issue. Will you take me?'

'Of course.' He sounded amenable enough about it. 'Make it tomorrow morning and we'll have lunch out, too. I'll have to be back before three, though, I'm expecting a call.'

'Did the South America deal fall through?' asked Leo suddenly. 'Or has it just been put back?'

'Let's just say we're negotiating terms. It could take time. I thought I might ride over to Scarsby market. It's been a long time since I had the opportunity.'

'Caroline is home,' Mrs Stafford remarked with the air of one imparting welcome information. 'Did you know?'

'I saw her this morning. She had that new hunter of her father's out.'

'Is she well?'

'Radiant.' His smile was slow, as if in recollection. 'Paris agrees with her. I'm going over there to dinner tonight, I'll tell her you asked.'

'Tell her to come on over to see me. I want to hear what she's been up to in Paris this last month. It's the next best thing to going oneself.' To Jessica she added, 'Did you ever visit Paris in the spring?'

'I've never visited Paris at all,' Jessica admitted. 'Though I'd certainly like to some day.'

'Not alone,' advised Leo lightly. 'It's a lovers' city.'

'Miss Chappel is disillusioned with love,' said Craig on a note of irony. 'She told me last night.'

'You surmised rather too much last night,' she countered, stifling the urge to say something really cutting. 'Actually, I told you nothing.'

'Except to mind my own business, which was a giveaway in itself!' He shook his head, mouth mocking. 'You certainly live up to your colouring.'

'It's almost the same as Beth's,' remarked Mrs Stafford, reaching for the salt. 'Isn't that a coincidence? And speaking of tempers, I've seen you lose yours before now.'

'Only when I've something to lose it over, and never in the boardroom. By the way, I had lunch with John Renfrew last week. He sends his regards.'

Jessica relaxed again slowly as the conversation moved on to safer ground. Not that anyone was really likely to guess the truth regardless. Looking up, she found Leo watching her with a quizzical expression and wondered what her face had given away. She would have to control her reactions better in future. After all, plenty of people had reddish hair.

It was Leo who made the first move after they finished eating, pushing back his chair to get to his feet.

'Miss Branston should be here by now,' he said. 'You'd better come and learn the worst.'

'Don't work her too hard on her first morning,' admonished his mother. 'I'll see you at lunch, Jessica.'

'Don't expect formality from anyone but Craig,' Leo advised on the way indoors. 'He thinks familiarity breeds contempt.'

'In some cases I'd agree with him,' she said lightly. 'It doesn't really matter what he chooses to call me, Leo. You're the one I'll be working with.'

'And Bob,' he reminded her. 'You'll get along fine with him. Everybody does.'

'Does he live on the estate?'

'Yes, there's a house goes with the job. What he doesn't know about running the place isn't worth knowing. There are twelve farms, for a start.'

The estate offices were out in the stable block at the side of the house. Later, Jessica was to learn that most of the block had been converted into garages, although these were rarely used in summer. Craig kept just two horses, being the only keen rider in the family. Cared for by a solitary groom, these were housed behind the main block with their own small yard and adjoining pasture.

Bob Grainger she liked on sight. He was a man in his late fifties, comfortably built and frankly balding. He smoked a pipe, and wore tweeds summer and winter alike, according to Leo. His greeting held a note of relief.

'I was beginning to think we were going to be left in the lurch,' he told her. 'Specially when you hadn't arrived by the time I went home last night. You'll find Miss Branston through in the other office. She'll tell you anything you want to know.'

The retiring secretary was a big-boned, plain woman in her mid-forties who made no secret of the fact that she regretted leaving her job.

'As the only daughter I'm the obvious one to look after Mother,' she confided over coffee, 'but I can't pretend to be overjoyed about it. I've been here three years and enjoyed every moment of it. Mr Grainger is a good man to work with.'

'And Mr Stafford?' Jessica asked lightly. 'How does he rate?'

'He's a gentleman—a real gentleman!' There was no doubting the sincerity of that tribute. 'He came to see me when he heard I was leaving—asked if it wouldn't be possible to arrange for nursing care for my mother so I could carry on here. He even offered to pay for it. I couldn't accept, of course. She wants me there, not some stranger. Still, it was good of him to think of it.'

'Very,' Jessica agreed, wondering if this could be the same man she had met. 'As a matter of fact, I was talking about Leo.'

'Oh, him!' The tone changed to one of intolerance. 'He's just a young layabout. All he thinks about is girls and cars and having a good time.'

'But he comes here to work, doesn't he?'

'He shows his face from time to time. Just occasionally he might even get round to signing a few cheques. If they're not payable to him he's not all that interested anyhow. Mr Grainger runs this estate on his own, you can take my word for that. You'll not even see the other one again before lunch.' Her smile was sour. 'Of course, when I've gone it might be a different story. You're young and attractive, and that's going to prove quite a draw. He might even be persuaded to start earning the salary he draws from the estate if you handle him the right way.'

'I'll do my best,' Jessica promised, 'but from what you tell me I doubt if it's going to make much difference once the novelty wears off. I'm here to work myself. I don't imagine I'm going to have too much time to spare.'

'There's enough to do,' the older woman agreed, 'but you'll cope all right. What puzzles me is why a girl your age should want to bury herself out here in the first place—especially coming from where you come from.'

Jessica smiled and shrugged. 'I needed a change of scene. And this is a lovely part of the country.'

'Well, we think so. Southerners usually find it a bit too bleak, especially up on the moors.' It was obvious that the other woman was not totally deceived. She briskened suddenly. 'Must get on. There's a lot to go through yet.'

The morning passed swiftly. When Leo put his head round the door Jessica was surprised to find it was already twelve-thirty.

'Lunch,' he said. 'I'll wait for you outside.'

Miss Branston shook her head when Jessica asked if she would be joining them.

'I've always brought sandwiches,' she said. 'I prefer it. You're living at the house, so it's different for you. I'd feel uncomfortable.'

Going out to where Leo waited, Jessica felt a pang of

sympathy for the woman she was leaving behind. Obviously not the gregarious type at the best of times, she was now being uprooted from the one secure little niche she had found. It seemed a bitter shame.

'So how's it going?' asked Leo on the way across to the house. 'Think you're going to cope?'

'Eventually,' she returned, and paused a moment before adding lightly, 'What happened to you all morning?'

'Oh, I was around.'

'The way you usually are?'

'Ah!' The exclamation was soft but not in any way rueful. 'The Gorgon's been telling tales out of school, has she? Well, it's quite true—I don't spend much time around the office. I'd be kicking my heels most of the day if I did.'

'You mean there isn't enough work for two of you?'

'I mean Bob prefers to do what there is to do himself, the way he's done for the last ten years. It's his whole life, managing Morley. He never learned how to delegate responsibility. Craig's idea was for me to take over and enable Bob to retire at sixty, only Bob doesn't want to retire at sixty.'

'Doesn't Craig know that?'

'Sure he knows it. Not that it makes any difference. He decides what's best for everybody. I suppose he considers that as he's stuck with me anyway he may as well make use of me.'

'Then leave,' Jessica suggested. 'Get a job and choose your own way of life.'

'How? I came down from Cambridge with little to show for it. You need a degree for any worthwhile job these days.'

'What about your brother? Surely he could find you something suitable.'

'You don't know Craig. He'd say if I wanted to stand on my own two feet then I should do it from scratch.'

'Coming from someone who inherited his own assets I'd say that was pretty unfair,' she commented.

'I agree, although to do him justice he's built up most of his outside interests himself. At present he runs two companies, and he's on the boards of several more.'

'Bully for him.' Now *she* was being unfair, Jessica thought, but it was how she felt. Damn Craig with his overbearing ways! Leo deserved a better deal than the one he'd got.

CHAPTER THREE

CRAIG was not present at lunch, but his great-uncle was. Now in his late seventies, Philip Stafford had retained a lean and upright figure along with a head of silvery hair. Last week's chill had left him pale and a little breathless, but his faculties were unimpaired.

'You remind me of someone,' he said to Jessica during the meal, 'only I can't quite place who.'

'It's the hair,' advised his niece, helping herself to more vegetables. 'It's almost the same colour as Beth's. We're going to have a couple of coppertops when she comes home.'

'When is she coming home?' he asked, successfully sidetracked. 'Surely she's had enough of Californian sunshine by now. In my day young women of her age were thinking about settling down, not gallivanting about the world!'

'It's because she was thinking about settling down that she is gallivanting about the world,' put in Leo with an air of deliberation. 'Craig hoped a few months away from it all might put it out of her mind. What he really means is Peter isn't good enough for a Stafford!'

'I'm sure that's not true,' his mother said soothingly. 'Peter is a very nice young man, and dedicated. Craig simply thinks Beth's too young to be married. Some girls of twenty are older than others.'

'And some have confidence in their own judgment because they've been allowed to form it,' came the rejoinder. 'Beth would make a good doctor's wife, given the chance. It's Craig who put the doubts in her mind.'

'He couldn't have done that if they weren't already there.'

Jessica kept her eyes on her plate, grateful that the conversation had turned away from her. This Peter they were discussing had to be the one she had met in the hotel last week; the coincidence was too much. She had left a note at the desk telling him of her sudden decision to return home, though without mentioning the reason why. Now she knew the cause of that look in his eyes when she had told him of her intention to visit Morley.

'What do you think, Jess?' Leo asked unexpectedly. 'Is twenty old enough for marriage?'

Jessica hated that abbreviation of her name, but thought it would seem churlish to say so. 'I suppose it has to depend,' she said. 'I agree with Mrs Stafford. Some girls mature quicker than others; I know I wouldn't have been ready to settle down at twenty.'

His grin was quick. 'How about twenty-three?'

She shook her head, refusing to rise. 'I'm not looking for a husband.'

'Career girls!' snorted Philip in mock disgust. 'What happened to femininity?'

'We still have it, Mr Stafford,' she retorted mildly, 'but we don't play on it as much. Most men need a wife who can meet them on an equal level these days.'

It was Leo's turn to snort. 'Not Craig. He'd love a good old-fashioned doormat! If Caroline played her cards right she'd have him hooked by now!'

Caroline again. Jessica tried idly to visualise the kind of woman who might attract Craig. She sounded like a blonde: a cool sophisticated blonde with expensive tastes. Obviously not one to relinquish her independence for a man, if what Leo said was true. And why should she?

Work finished for the day around four, leaving Jessica free to make her way back to the house. Leo was coming down the stairs as she went up, legs bare beneath a towelling robe.

'I'm just off for a swim,' he announced. 'Why don't you come too? This fine spell's due to break tomorrow.'

After a day indoors the suggestion was tempting. 'I didn't bring a suit,' she said with regret.

'No problem—I'll get one of Beth's. You're about the same size.' He was gone before she could reply.

The knock on her door came only bare moments after she had reached the room. Leo pressed a robe much like his own into her hands, along with a black bikini. 'I wasn't sure whether you'd have one of these either,' he said. 'Beth won't mind. I'll be out on the terrace when you're ready. We can have tea when we get back.'

The bikini was the briefest Jessica had ever worn, but it fitted like a glove. Looking at herself in the long dressing mirror, she knew a momentary doubt, swiftly squashed. She had a good enough figure to get away with it, so why the reticence? True, a tan might have enhanced things, but gaining a decent one without burning was such a toil for anyone her colouring. Beth no doubt suffered the same lack of pigment, which hardly made California the ideal place to spend any length of time.

This similarity between them was hardly so surprising considering the fact that titian hair ran in the Stafford family. Grandmother had had it, so had her own mother, and several of the portraits on the stairs revealed varying shades of red. Craig even had a hint of it himself, although in his case the skin tone was obviously tempered by his mother's genes. She wondered if he was back yet.

It took only a couple of minutes to walk down to the lake from the house. There was a wooden jetty with a small rowing boat moored beneath it. Leo led the way out to the end, shedding his robe as he went. He had a fine body, Jessica acknowledged: lean and lithe and smoothly bronzed. He knew it too. It was there in the way he moved, the way he held himself. Fate had been kind to him when it came to sheer, downright good looks.

She felt a little selfconscious taking off her own robe in front of him, but the frank approval in his glance was a boost in itself.

'It's deep enough to dive from here,' he said. 'Are you a good swimmer?'

'Good enough.' She had tied back her hair from her face at the house. Now she kicked off her sandals and moved to the edge of the jetty. 'I'll race you across.'

'You're on!' He was at her side, eyes sparkling to the challenge. 'Let's go!'

They hit the water almost simultaneously, surfacing to go straight into a fast racing crawl. Swimming was one sport at which Jessica excelled. She had no difficulty in keeping pace with her opponent, and at one point began to draw ahead until he put on an unexpected spurt to finish half a length in front.

'You weren't kidding, were you?' he gasped as they drew themselves out on to the grassy bank to take a breather before heading back. 'I had all on to keep up with you. Do you always play to win?'

'I didn't win,' Jessica pointed out without rancour. 'I have to give best.'

'I wouldn't put it past you to have let me win,' he said, grinning up at her from his prone position. 'You're the kind of girl who'd take a man's pride into consideration.'

'Don't count on it.' She stood up, squeezing water from the ends of her hair. 'Shall we get back? I'm ready for that tea.'

'You're a glutton for punishment!' Leo groaned, but he pushed himself upright. 'Okay, but take it easy this time. The old body can't take too much.'

The return journey was accomplished at a leisurely pace that gave the adrenalin time to settle. Nevertheless,

Jessica for one could feel the pull on her muscles by the time they made it to home shore. The race had been foolish without a warm-up first. She would pay for it in the morning when she woke up stiff and sore.

Leo was first out of the water in the shallows at the side of the jetty, holding out a helping hand as Jessica stumbled over the slippery stones and yanking her upright. The kiss was swift and light, bestowed on her lifted mouth as she started to thank him.

'Tribute to a gallant loser,' he said, blue eyes laughing. 'Anyway, I've been wanting to do that all day!'

Jessica made no answer, looking beyond him to the horse and rider moving across her line of vision towards the house. Craig must have seen them; he couldn't fail to have seen them. To an onlooker it might well appear that she had invited that kiss.

So what? she asked herself hardily. Leo had just been fooling around. It hadn't meant anything. If Craig didn't realise that it was just too bad.

They were on the terrace drinking the tea Pauline had brought out to them when he appeared from the direction of the stables. The jodhpurs and hacking jacket suited him, Jessica found herself thinking irrelevantly. He had the right kind of legs for boots too, long in the calf. Something tautened ominously inside her.

'Any of that going spare?' asked Craig, pulling out a chair.

There were spare cups on the trolley. Jessica poured a third without being asked, placing it at his elbow on the table.

'Sandwich?' she enquired.

He shook his head without looking at her. 'No, thanks, I'll wait till dinner. How was the water?'

'Invigorating,' his brother replied with lazy inflection. 'This girl can swim like a fish. She almost had me beat!'

'Really?' The interest was of the polite kind. 'That must have given you something to think about.' Still without looking at Jessica he added, 'Did Miss Branston show you everything you needed to know?'

'Just about,' she said. 'There's still tomorrow.'

'No, there isn't. I called in on Bob Grainger on the way back, and she'd just phoned through to say she didn't feel up to coming in tomorrow.'

'Too upset, I imagine.' There was sympathy in Jessica's voice. 'She didn't want to leave Morley.'

'Yes, it's unfortunate. Do you think you can cope?'

'Of course.' She said it with confidence. 'There's nothing complicated about the paper work, only a lot of it. Once I get my own system going I'll be fine.'

This time he did look at her, a hard look. 'You're saying hers wasn't efficient?'

'No.' She kept her tone level. 'Simply different. We all have our own ways.'

'And opinions.' Leo finished his tea at a single gulp and came to his feet. 'I'm going up to change. Coming, Jess?'

'Miss Chappel is staying here,' said Craig without inflection. 'I want to talk to her.'

'About work? Surely that can wait!'

'You go ahead, Leo,' Jessica put in swiftly, seeing his brother's face darken. 'I haven't finished my tea yet anyway.'

There was a lengthy silence after the young man had left the room. Craig was the first to break it.

'Have you forgotten what I said last night, or just choosing to ignore it?'

'That depends,' she said, 'on what it is I'm supposed to remember. You said rather a lot last night.'

'Don't prevaricate with me,' he growled. 'You know damned well what I'm talking about. I told you to stay clear of my brother!'

'But you forgot to tell him to stay clear of me,' she

rejoined. 'Not that it's necessary. He's simply being friendly.'

'Very, from what I saw down by the lake!'

'What you saw down by the lake was one of those spur-of-the-moment things that doesn't mean a thing,' she came back, still without raising her voice above normal conversational level. 'Didn't you ever give way to an impulse just because someone happened to be there at the right moment?'

'And asking for it,' he tagged on sardonically.

'That's not true!' This time her tone was sharper. 'You're reading too much into too little!'

'I'll be the judge of that.' The pause was measured. 'I'll say it once more. Leave Leo alone.'

'He's twenty-four,' Jessica pointed out. 'Don't you think you're being a little over-protective?'

'I'm not prepared to argue about it. Either take notice or . . .'

'Or take notice,' she finished for him with irony. 'I'm not sure you'd have adequate grounds for dismissal. Most courts would accept that your brother was capable of looking after his own interests.'

Grey eyes narrowed suddenly and dangerously. 'Are you threatening me?'

'Just making a point.' She could hardly credit her own calmness. 'You can't run everyone's lives for them. Even your little sister should be allowed a mind of her own.'

Craig said grimly, 'Just what has Leo been telling you?'

'As a matter of fact it was your great-uncle who started it,' she denied. 'He apparently wants her home. I imagine Dr Turner does too.'

The tensing of a muscle along the line of his jaw was the only reaction visible. 'I think you'd better go and get changed,' he advised. 'You've gone as far as you're going to go.'

Too far for an employee, Jessica had to concede. She had been speaking from an inside position—already involved more than she should be with this family and its problems. She knew she should apologise, but the words wouldn't come.

'Did you hear what I said?' He was quiet, and all the more meaningful for it. 'You can go.'

She got up without haste, nerves finely stretched. There was an odd kind of excitement in standing her ground where Craig Stafford was concerned, but there had to be limits. If she didn't want to find herself thrown out of the house she had to keep remembering that he was her employer and entitled to some modicum of respect. After less than twenty-four hours at Morley she knew she didn't want to leave the place. It was as if, through her, Grandmother had finally come home again.

She took care to keep out of Craig's way over the following couple of days, which wasn't too difficult as he showed little inclination to be in her company either. On Saturday, Leo insisted on taking her into Skipton, driving the red Ferrari with style and panache.

'One of my few extravagances,' he claimed over tea in a café close by the church. 'It costs a small fortune just to keep her tuned, but she's worth it!'

'Why do men always call their cars she?' asked Jessica lightly.

He grinned. 'Because they're beautiful, unpredictable and expensive to maintain—I'd have thought it obvious. Next weekend I'll take you to the coast. You said you wanted to visit Whitby. Do you know someone there?'

She shook her head. 'I used to know someone who talked a lot about the place. My guide book calls it unspoiled and unchanged.'

'I don't suppose it has changed a lot,' Leo agreed. 'Not in my time anyway. Fishing's still the main industry. We'll make it a full day. I know a great little spot for dinner on the way back.'

Jessica hesitated before saying it, aware that he wasn't going to like it. 'Your brother warned me to stay away from you outside of working hours.' She tried to lighten the words with a touch of humour. 'I think he believes I have designs on you.'

'And do you?' The tone was mock-serious.

'No,' she said frankly. 'You're no more my type than I am yours. Anyway, judging from the number of girls you seem to be on intimate terms with I'd just be one of a crowd. Who was the pretty brunette in the blue dress?'

'Deirdre Hanson. Her father's a local publican.' Blue eyes looked back at her innocently. 'We're just good friends.'

'Which is why she looked so totally stricken when she saw you with another girl, I suppose?' Jessica shook her head, half smiling, half reproving. 'You've probably broken more hearts than you can count.'

'Only bent a few. I never let things get too serious.'

'You mean at twenty-four you've never once felt the pangs of genuine love?' she teased.

Just for a moment his smile flickered, then he was laughing and shaking his head. 'I don't believe in suffering.' There was a pause and a sudden change of mood, his voice taking on a new note. 'You aren't going to let Craig dictate what you do in your own time, are you, because I'm certainly not. We can be friends without having to have an affair.' The wicked sparkle returned for a moment. 'Mind you, I might not be able to stop myself from kissing you now and then. You have the most irresistible mouth.'

'You'll have to work on your willpower,' she retorted. 'Do you realise it's almost five?'

'So what? There's nothing to rush back for. I thought we might go into Leeds now we're this close and take in a film.'

Bother Craig, Jessica told herself in sudden recklessness. Leo was right: why should he be allowed to lay down the law? She and Leo were both adults. They would make their own decisions.

Leo's 'close' proved to be a matter of thirty miles or so. It was gone seven when they got into the cinema and around ten when they came out again. Jessica turned down his suggestion of a late supper somewhere, reckoning it was already going to be after eleven by the time they made it back to Morley. Not exactly late for a Saturday evening perhaps, but they had been gone since lunchtime.

The house was still lit like a Christmas tree when they reached it. Craig's silver-grey Mercedes was standing outside the front door as if in readiness. He came out from the drawing room as they went indoors, a slender blonde-haired young woman at his side. The expression in the grey eyes boded ill for someone.

'I told you Caroline was coming over to dinner tonight,' he said grimly to Leo. 'The least you could have done was be here.'

'Forgot all about it.' The younger man's tone held little real repentance. 'Sorry, Caroline. How was Paris?'

'Wonderful!' The smile lent warmth and life to the finely modelled features. Her gaze shifted to Jessica. 'You must be Miss Chappel.'

'Her name is Jessica,' Leo put in before she could answer. 'Only Craig calls her Miss Chappel. Caroline Paige, our next-door neighbour.'

'Hardly next door.' The smile was still there. 'We're two miles away. What do you think of Yorkshire?'

'What I've seen of it so far I like,' Jessica acknowledged, trying not to let her gaze wander to Craig's face. 'Three days is hardly long enough to get acquainted.'

'What about a drink?' suggested Leo. 'It's too early to turn in.'

Craig shook his head. 'I was just about to take Caroline home.'

'That's a shame.' Leo refused to be dampened. 'We'll just have to drink alone, Jess.'

'I'm rather tired,' she said. 'I think I'll go straight on up, if you don't mind.' Her smile encompassed them all. 'Goodnight.'

Leo made no attempt to follow her, much to her relief. It would have been like him to deliberately add fuel to the fire. She doubted if Craig was going to be content to leave it there even so ... She had defied his orders; he wasn't going to like that. Yet what could he really do about it, when all was said and done? As Leo had said, he had no control over her free time.

She was in bed before the pangs of hunger began making themselves felt to any great degree. Going too long without a proper meal had been foolish, she acknowledged, especially when tea had consisted of a couple of small scones and jam. Ten to one Leo would not have gone to bed hungry. It was only just gone midnight, which meant another eight hours at least before breakfast. Right now it seemed an eternity.

By half past twelve she could stand it no longer, and threw back the covers to reach for her thin cotton wrap. Come what may, she had to find something to eat, or at least a drink of milk, otherwise she was going to get little sleep.

The house was in darkness. She didn't bother putting on a light, finding her way by that from the windows. She had only once seen inside the kitchen, but had noted the two large refrigerators. There was sure to be some cold meat she could slice for a sandwich, or perhaps a chicken joint left over from lunch. She didn't much care what it was.

By night the big white gleaming kitchen had an eerie quality. With her sandwich of cold roast beef made and a glass of milk poured, Jessica decided to return to the warm familiarity of her own room where she could relax over her midnight feast. Carrying the glass in one hand and the plate in the other, she was forced to use an elbow to depress the handle of the door leading from the back passage into the hall, pushing with a hip as she did so in order to open it, then sliding away so that the sprung closing arm could do its job.

The sudden switching on of a light froze her to the spot, arms rigidly extended either side as she stared blankly at the man over by the main doors. Craig had apparently just come in, his suit jacket over his arm, collar open at the throat above the loosened tie. He was the first to speak.

'Couldn't Leo afford to feed you tonight?'

Jessica made an effort to collect herself, without very much success. She felt foolish and juvenile, like some schoolgirl caught raiding the pantry for goodies she wasn't supposed to have.

'We didn't get round to dinner,' she explained. 'It was too late when we came out of the cinema.'

'In Leeds?' His brows lifted fractionally. 'Cinemas turn out around ten. I can think of at least a dozen places you could have eaten—or did you have other things on your mind right then?'

'If you like.' Head up, she moved towards the stairs. 'Goodnight, Mr Stafford.'

He came after her silently and swiftly, taking both plate and glass from her hands to deposit them on a convenient surface before swinging to confront her. With his jacket slung over a broad shoulder and his hair ruffled as if from the passage of a hand through it, he looked different. For the first time Jessica acknowledged his attraction, her stomach muscles tense. She could hardly bring herself to meet his eyes.

'Why are you here?' he demanded. 'The real reason.'

'I've already told you.' Her heart was thudding

against her ribs so hard she thought he must hear it. 'I needed a change. It was pure chance that I happened to visit here at a time when a job was coming open.'

'And in a few minutes you'd made a decision to move from one end of the country to the other?' He was openly sceptical. 'I might have been easier to convince if you'd shown even a passing interest in what would normally be the most crucial question.' The pause was timed. 'Tell me, what salary are you getting?'

Jessica bit her lip, aware that he had her there. Salary had been the last thing on her mind this past week or so. 'Your brother told me you'd top my previous salary,' she said at length. 'It seemed a satisfactory offer.'

'Providing he knew what your previous salary was, which he doesn't, because I've asked him. Care to try again?'

Now was the time to tell him the simple truth, but she couldn't bring herself to do it. She took refuge instead in anger, eyes stormy. 'All right, so I fell for Leo the moment I saw him and just had to be near him! Does that satisfy you?'

'Hardly.' He was quite unmoved. 'You're not the type to let your heart rule your head.'

'You don't know me,' she retorted. 'You've no idea what I might be capable of. If I was really as calculating as you're making out, I'd hardly have set my sights on the younger brother, would I? It would have been the master of the house or nothing!'

'True,' he agreed with the same infuriating calm. 'But then, knowing my brother, it's quite possible he let you think he *was* the master of the house.' He was silent for a moment, his eyes never leaving her face. When he spoke again it was on a different note. 'There's something about you that bothers me, Jessica Chappel— something I can't quite put my finger on. We've never met before, have we?'

'No.' Her heart was in her throat now, the dryness painful. 'I'd never even heard of you until I came here.'

'The lady doth protest too much, methinks,' he quoted softly. 'If we accept the fact that you're not after Leo, what else could there be?'

It was impossible that he should guess the truth, of course, yet it was that very fear which jerked her into response. 'If you must know, you're partially right. I'm here because of a man.' She drew in a steadying breath, forcing herself to hold his gaze. 'I—we were going to be married and he changed his mind.' It was only half a truth, but more plausible than the whole. 'We worked for the same company. That's why I left.'

There was no telling whether he believed her or not. 'Surely changing your job would have been enough.'

'We moved in the same circles,' she improvised quickly. 'It was bad enough seeing him at all, but——'

'But seeing him with another girl was even worse,' he finished for her as she hesitated. 'You might have got over it all the faster if you'd stuck it out.'

'Except that I don't have that kind of courage.' She was getting the feel of the role now, pride rearing. 'I prefer to lick my wounds in private—when I'm allowed to.'

Craig was looking at her with an odd expression. 'You're a very attractive young woman. You shouldn't have any difficulty finding yourself another husband.'

'Providing it isn't your brother.' She shook her head. 'Even if I had been that way inclined it wouldn't have been any use. Leo isn't interested in me.'

'He kissed you the other day.'

'Only because that's how he is. He'd kiss any girl who happened to be within kissing distance. You were the only one who took it seriously.'

'So it seems.' For the first time Craig allowed his gaze to move downwards over her, giving her a sudden urge to clutch the wrap tightly about her. 'You'd better get to bed,' was all he said. 'Can you manage your snack, or shall I bring it up?'

'I can manage.' She took up the plate and glass and turned away from him, forcing herself to move without haste when every nerve in her wanted to hurry out of his way. 'Goodnight again.'

He didn't answer, mounting the stairs a little way behind her. The cotton wrap was long, getting in the way of her feet as she lifted them to each tread. Inadvertently she stumbled, the milk slopping over the edges of the glass as her arm jerked. The hands coming around her waist from the rear were firm and warm, steadying her balance. She could feel him behind her, so close his breath stirred the hair at the back of her neck.

'You'd better give me the plate, then you can lift that thing out of the way,' he said. 'Otherwise you're going to finish up breaking something less easily repairable than a heart.' One hand left her to come over her shoulder and take the plate from her, the other lingering for a brief moment longer before urging her gently forward. 'Go on, you're safe enough now.'

Was she? Jessica wondered, nervelessly obeying the injunction. She had never felt less so. Craig's touch had stirred her senses the way Brian's had never done. She wanted him to take hold of her again, to feel those strong hands turning her towards him, see his mouth descending to hers. Crazy, of course. If Leo had little emotional interest in her, his brother had even less. He would probably be amused to know how he affected her—if he didn't already know. A man like Craig would not be dense when it came to sensing response in a woman. No doubt he had felt it through his very fingertips.

Their ways divided when they came to the head of the staircase, hers to the left and his to the right along the open gallery. Jessica took the plate from him without raising her head, conscious of the flatness of his stomach beneath the well-cut trousers, the relative slimness of his hips. That same configuration in Leo had aroused only admiration, not this tingling awareness.

'I'm leaving in the morning,' he told her, 'so I shan't be seeing you for a week or so. If I've misjudged you, I apologise.'

'It doesn't matter.' Her voice sounded strange and far-away. 'A business trip?'

'The same one I put off. They've come up with a new deal.' There was a moment when he seemed about to add something else, then he shrugged and began to move away. 'Goodnight, Jessica.'

CHAPTER FOUR

FOR Jessica the week following passed quickly and pleasantly enough. She liked her job, loved her surroundings and found plenty to occupy her spare time even without Leo's help.

Louise Stafford proved an invaluable companion in the evenings, only too pleased to have someone outside of immediate family to talk with.

'There was a time when the house used to be full of Leo's friends and aquaintances,' she said on one occasion, 'but they stopped coming—or he stopped inviting them, I'm not sure which. I quite miss them, although some of them weren't exactly our kind.' Her smile was faintly wry. 'I'm basically against nonconformation, especially where common cleanliness takes a back seat.'

'I suppose Leo outgrew them,' Jessica observed casually. 'A lot go through that stage. I think it's called finding oneself.'

'Craig didn't, thank heaven. He had to accept a lot of responsibility when his father died. Leo was only thirteen at the time, and Beth a mere child, so he had to be father as well as brother. That's why he's so protective now.' She paused to pick up a dropped stitch, frowning in concentration. 'Got it! What was I saying? Oh, yes, Beth. I suppose a lot of girls do marry at her age, but Peter is hardly in a position to provide her with the standard of living she's accustomed to.'

'But if she loves him,' Jessica said softly, 'surely that makes a difference?'

'Does it? I'm not so sure. Oh, initially perhaps, when everything is fresh and new, but what about later when the novelty wears off?' She shook her head. 'I have to agree with Craig. Give it a couple of years before she starts to think about settling down. From the tone of her letters she's beginning to see the sense in that too.'

Poor Peter, Jessica reflected. When the Staffords closed ranks no outsider stood a chance. Leo had seemed sympathetic, though, she recalled—or had that simply been his way of kicking against his brother's dictum? He stood in such a no-man's-land here at Morley. Better by far if he moved out from under Craig's shadow and started living his own life.

'Have you thought about your costume for the Ball yet?' asked Mrs Stafford unexpectedly. 'It's little more than a week away.'

It was a moment before Jessica answered. 'I wasn't sure I was invited.'

'Of course you're invited!' The older woman sounded surprised. 'What did you think we were going to do with you—tell you to stay out for the night? You do realise it's masquerade?'

'No, I didn't.' Jessica paused, recalling a certain conversation with puzzlement. 'You said you were ordering your dress from a Harrod's style. I didn't know they catered for masquerade.'

'I doubt if they do,' came the comfortable response. 'I simply refuse to wear fancy dress. The rest of you have to—it's traditional. There's a very good dress-hire place in Harrogate. Saturday is going to be your last opportunity to find something suitable if you can't come up with any ideas of your own. Do you have a flair for that sort of thing?'

'I've never tried,' Jessica admitted. 'I doubt it.' She hesitated, oddly reluctant to even say the name. 'Does Craig go along with tradition too?'

'He wouldn't dare break it.' The smile was reminiscent. 'Last year he leaned on my Scottish ancestry and came as a Highland chieftain in full

Stewart tartan. He has the legs for it, of course. Some men look ridiculous in the kilt. Anyway, you think about it. As I said, you don't have too much time.'

Jessica used the same phrase to Leo on Friday evening when he reminded her of their proposed excursion to the coast the following day.

'There's no other time I can get into town,' she added. 'I can hardly wait until the day of the ball and trust to luck that they'll have something to fit me. What will you be going as, anyway?'

'It's a secret,' he said. 'We mask until midnight, just to add to the fun. Some costumes make it difficult to tell who the wearer is. I remember a couple of years back I spent most of the night chasing after a little Dresden shepherdess, only to find it was Beth in a powdered wig!'

Jessica laughed. 'What a let-down!'

'Yes, it was. Not that I saw the humorous side of it at the time. I could have throttled her for not letting on. You should have seen the act she put on!'

'Your sister sounds a character,' she commented. 'Did you hear yet when she might be coming home?'

'No, but I can't see her staying away from the Ball. She'll probably just turn up some time next week.' He reverted to the original subject. 'We can't make it Sunday, I've something else on. I suppose we'll just have to shelve it for the moment. I'll run you into Harrogate, though.'

She said quickly, 'I'd rather go alone—I've quite a lot of shopping to do. You'd hardly enjoy trailing around after me.'

He made no attempt to deny it. 'Be independent, then. I daresay I can fill my day.'

With Deirdre Hanson? Jessica wondered. The girl couldn't be more than seventeen, and if the look on her face last week was anything to go by she was already head over heels where Leo was concerned. His policy of never allowing things to get too serious apparently only extended itself one way. One could only hope that the girl wouldn't be too badly hurt when the time came.

Harrogate on a Saturday morning proved busier even than she anticipated. She had difficulty in parking the car, and even more in finding the address Mrs Stafford had supplied.

From the front the shop looked small and a trifle shabby, but the interior was freshly decorated. Once having elicited the fact that Jessica had few ideas of her own, the proprietor brought out a book listing dozens of costumes and suggested she choose three or four likely ones to try on. All garments were dry-cleaned between hirings, he assured her with the air of one who was often asked that particular question.

Of the four choices she finally made, only one showd any real promise. It was an Empress line dress in a soft blue material which looked and felt like heavy satin, the low square neckline edged with tiny seed pearls. With her hair taken up and supplemented by a surprisingly well-matched cluster of ringlets she looked every inch the Empress Josephine, said the proprietor, fetching his wife from the back to admire the effect.

The neckline caused Jessica a few misgivings, but not enough to put her off completely. It was either this or start all over again with four more choices, and even then with no guarantee that she was going to find one to fit as well.

'Would it be possible to take it with me now?' she asked. 'I don't really want to make another trip into town next week. It's Morley Grange,' she added by way of explanation. 'A bit too far to keep popping in and out.'

'We can deliver the costume next Saturday morning along with those for both Mr Staffords,' offered the man. 'That way you'll only be paying for a weekend hire. You'll need a mask too if it's the Morley ball.

They do it the traditional way.' He sounded approving. 'Staying there, are you, miss?'

'Working there,' she corrected. 'I'm the new estate secretary.'

'Yes, well, it's a grand place to be. Well respected family, the Staffords.' He handed over a receipt for the hiring fee, interest switching abruptly to the new customer just entering the shop. 'Can I help you, sir?'

'I'm after a masquerade costume,' said the newcomer, coming forward to the counter. 'Something fairly simple, I think.' He paused there, looking sideways at Jessica as she tucked away the receipt in her purse in sudden recognition. 'This is a surprise! I thought you'd gone back to London?'

Jessica turned her head to look at the young doctor with a feeling that fate was once again taking a hand in her life. 'Hallo again,' she smiled. 'I didn't expect to see you either, although I suppose I should have done, considering you live here. You obviously got my message all right.'

'Yes, I did. You didn't say anything about coming back.'

'I wasn't a hundred per cent sure I would be at the time. I—it all happened rather fast.'

'It must have, whatever it was.' He made a decisive movement. 'Look, it's gone twelve already. Why don't we have some lunch, then I can come back here this afternoon.' To the man behind the counter he added, 'You are open all day, aren't you?'

'Two till five.' There was a lively speculation in the watching eyes. 'Something simple, you said? I'll have a look through the book and see what we've got.'

'There's a very good little restaurant a couple of doors away,' Peter advised when they were outside. 'You do have time for lunch?'

'Oh yes,' Jessica laughed. 'As a matter of fact, I was wondering where to go.'

'Well, now you can leave it to Uncle Peter.'

He waited until they were seated in the small but well-appointed restaurant and their meal ordered before giving way to curiosity. 'What are you really doing here in Harrogate? You told me you were on holiday before.'

'So I was,' she said. 'It was pure coincidence that I found out about this job going at Morley, and too good an opportunity to miss.'

'You're working at Morley?' He sounded taken aback. 'Doing what?'

'Estate secretary. I replaced a Miss Branston.'

'Oh, yes, I heard she'd left. It just never occurred to me that you might be her successor.' He paused, eyeing her thoughtfully. 'How do you like it?'

'Fine.' She kept her tone light. 'Mrs Stafford has gone out of her way to make me feel at home.'

'So has Leo, I imagine,' he came back dryly. 'What about Craig?'

'He hasn't been there most of the time.' Jessica congratulated herself on the lack of inflection in her voice. 'I haven't got to meet the daughter yet either. She's away in California, by all accounts.'

'She'll be back before the Ball.' He said it with confidence. He studied her for a moment, a faint smile touching his lips. 'You know about us, don't you?'

Obviously her control of expression was not as good as she imagined, Jessica acknowledged ruefully. 'Did I make it that plain?'

'You were too deadpan—or maybe I'm just over-sensitive where Beth is concerned.' He paused again. 'What exactly did you hear?'

Her shrug was uncomfortable. 'Simply that Craig was standing in the way of your marriage.'

'He's attempted to. It won't work because I shan't let it work. Neither will Beth.'

'You've heard from her?'

The determination in his eyes faded just a little. 'Not too recently,' he admitted, 'but it doesn't mean anything. Beth was never much for letter-writing. She won't have changed, though, I can vouch for that.'

Remembering what Mrs Stafford had said only the other evening, Jessica wondered if his confidence was a little misplaced. It was hardly her place, however, to say so. 'I gather you're going to the Ball too,' she said instead.

'As the family G.P. I have a standing invitation,' Peter admitted. 'My great-grandfather convinced them they were in good hands in the twenties, and they've stuck with the Turner medics ever since, for general purposes, at least.'

'It must be fairly unusual for four successive generations to take up medicine,' Jessica commented. 'Did you ever feel like breaking loose yourself?'

Peter shook his head. 'I've wanted to be a doctor since I was old enough to hold a stethoscope. I just thank my lucky stars I had the brains to make it.'

Jessica enjoyed the hour or so they took over lunch, but wasn't too surprised when he failed to suggest a repetition. Her colouring might have provided the draw that very first morning, but she wasn't Beth and never could be. She silently wished him luck in his coming reunion with the girl he loved.

She was back at the house by three, her equilibrium totally destroyed by the sight of the car parked out front. Craig was home again sooner than anticipated. She felt unprepared to see him; ill-equipped to handle the confusion of emotion he aroused in her. They had parted on fairly amicable terms, but there was no knowing what his present attitude might be.

George was in the process of discussing the portraits on the stairs as he escorted a small party of sightseers upwards. One or two of the latter looked down at Jessica curiously when she came in through the big main doors, following her with their eyes as she crossed the tiled floor to mount the first short flight of stairs and start to remove the rope barrier in order to pass through.

'Jessica!' The voice came from the drawing room door. 'I thought I heard your car. Come on down again, dear, there's someone I want you to meet.'

Slowly, conscious of the interest aroused in the visiting party, Jessica obeyed, moving across to where Mrs Stafford stood waiting.

'I was just taking these upstairs,' she said, indicating her various small parcels. 'That is Mr Stafford's car outside, isn't it?'

'It is, and he brought someone with him.' Taking her arm, the older woman drew her forward and into the lovely blue and gold room. 'My daughter Beth—Jessica Chappel. I'm sure you two girls are going to get along just fine.'

The girl seated in one of the elegant Louis XV chairs adjoining the Adam fireplace looked as wary as Jessica felt. She appeared even younger than her years, the devastatingly pretty face topped by a riot of titian curls. Despite her colouring, her skin was tanned to a shade that aroused Jessica's envy, the effect nicely enhanced by the white denim pants and jacket she wore.

'Hi,' she said.

'Hallo.' Jessica scarcely knew what else to add. Involuntarily her eyes were drawn to the tall figure standing easily in front of the fireplace with an elbow at rest on the mantel, heart jerking to the impact of his regard. There was something in the line of his mouth that suggested derision—or was that just imagination on her part? She said the first thing that came into her head. 'I thought it was South America you were visiting?'

'It's the same continent,' he returned without moving. 'I only needed to spend a couple of days sorting out the situation in Caracas, so I took the opportunity of calling in to collect some excess baggage.'

'Baggage yourself!' retorted his sister inelegantly. 'I was ready to come home anyway. You didn't think I was going to miss the July Ball, did you? I even brought my costume with me.'

'That's perhaps as well, considering you didn't leave yourself very much time to organise anything here.' Mrs Stafford glanced at Jessica. 'Did you get fixed up?'

'Yes.' For the life of her Jessica could think of nothing to add to that statement.

'Well, we'll look forward to seeing it on the night,' the older woman said comfortably. 'Incidentally, I may have found a housekeeper. I had a letter from Dulcie Renfrew this morning. They're turning Copley over to the National Trust and moving to the Lodge, which means Mrs Forsyth will be looking for another post. What do you think, Craig? I really can't cope on my own for very much longer.'

'That's entirely up to you,' he said. 'Find out what salary she was getting at Copley and make her an offer, if you think she'd be suitable. I refuse to be involved with hiring household staff.'

'I thought you'd say that,' she sighed. 'You know how I hate making decisions. Mrs Forsyth is efficient, I know, but a bit of the dour Scot. I'm not sure how she'd fit in. What's your opinion, Jessica?'

The appeal startled her, coming as it did out of the blue. She shot a glance at Craig, but received no help there. He too seemed to be waiting to hear what she had to say.

'I'm hardly qualified to have one,' she got out at length. 'Not on that subject. I'd say you'd probably lose Pauline if this Mrs Forsyth turned out to be too much of a martinet, but you could always find another maid.'

'Not easily,' Mrs Stafford admitted. 'Not in these parts. Girls don't want to go into service these days. I'll have to think about it a little more before I do anything concrete.'

'We should copy the Americans,' put in Beth airily. 'Helen and Ritchie just have the one couple who do everything. Of course, *they* don't live in a museum!'

'Neither do you,' responded her brother equably, 'though I'll agree it's a little larger than Ritchie's place. Actually, a couple wouldn't be a bad idea. The man could combine chauffeuring with his other duties, then I wouldn't have to keep running your mother into town.' His smile robbed the words of any serious intent. 'Contact the agencies again and put it to them.' He straightened away from the mantelshelf, his glance going to the window. 'Feel like a ride, Beth?'

'Not right now,' she said. 'I shouldn't have thought you'd have the energy after driving all the way from Heathrow.'

'It's the best way I know of relaxing.' Grey eyes swung in Jessica's direction. 'How about you? I meant to tell you to make full use of both animals before I left.'

'I don't ride,' she admitted, feeling inadequate. 'The only time I've even been on a horse was at a fair a couple of years ago, and that wasn't too successful.' She smiled wryly. 'It just stopped dead half way round this track they'd rigged up and refused to budge. In the end they had to send someone out to lead me in again.'

'Sounds like my first pony,' Beth acknowledged on a note of sympathy. 'They recognise the weak-willed right away. You should learn while you're here—Craig's a good teacher. You can borrow some of my gear. I bet we even take the same shoe size.'

'I don't think . . .' Jessica began doubtfully, and was interrupted by Craig's decisive movement.

'There's no time like the present. Fix her up, Beth. I'll get changed myself and see you down in the stable yard in about fifteen minutes. Oh, Mother, before I go . . .'

'Better get a move on,' Beth advised with laughing eyes, moving towards the door. 'He doesn't like being kept waiting.'

Her bedroom was at the rear of the house only a couple of doors from Jessica's own. In addition to the en-suite bathroom, there was also an adjoining dressing area lined with glass-doored wardrobes. Beth opened one of the latter to reveal a sizeable selection of riding gear, including four pairs of boots.

'Size twelve, and a five shoe, yes?' she said. 'I thought we were a similar build.' She took down a pair of jodhpurs and the nearest of the boots. 'These should do. You'll need a sweater.'

Jessica took the things from her a little uncomfortably. 'Thanks,' she said. 'It's generous of you to offer.'

'Oh, that's okay. Keep them until you know whether it's going to be worthwhile buying any of your own. You might turn out to hate horses—especially after Craig's finished putting you through your paces. Dumb animals merit more patience than humans. Believe me, if you fall off he'll make sure the horse is all right before getting round to you.'

Jessica had to laugh despite herself. 'You're just trying to give me confidence, aren't you?'

'Something like that.' Beth gave her an appraising look. 'I must say, you're an improvement on Miss Branston! Perhaps as well, seeing you're living in. Mummy was singing your praises before you came back. She said you and she had had some delightful evenings. The poor darling doesn't get too much attention paid her by either Leo or me, I have to admit, and Craig isn't too often here.'

'I like your mother,' Jessica acknowledged. 'She's a very easy person to be with. Now, I'd better go and get into these.'

'Yes, you had. You're running out of time. By the

way,' Beth added as Jessica reached the door, 'you don't happen to know where Leo went, do you?'

Jessica shook her head. 'He didn't tell me.'

'Oh well, it doesn't really matter.' The other girl's tone was brightly casual. 'Something I wanted to ask him, that's all.'

About Peter Turner? Jessica wondered on the way to her room. From the look of her, Beth hadn't exactly been pining away, but then who could tell what went on inside a person? First impressions, however, did not suggest a girl ready for marriage, especially to a man who would need a wife capable of rising to any occasion that might offer itself. She could begin to understand Craig's doubts.

Both jodhpurs and boots fitted her comfortably. Feeling a little selfconscious, she made her way downstairs again and out through the rear premises. Both horses were out and ready saddled when she reached the stables. Craig was checking the leathers. The glance he gave her was cursory.

'You'll be riding Dorian here—he's quiet enough. Do you need a leg up?'

'I'd imagine so,' said Jessica, eyeing the height of the stirrup iron dubiously. 'I'm going to have difficulty even getting my foot up there.'

'That attitude isn't going to get you far.' The scorn was underlined. 'Get a hold of the reins and the front of the saddle and bend your left knee a little.' He put a hand lightly under it as she obeyed. 'Now, as I lift you spring with it. Up you go!'

Somehow Jessica found herself seated more or less securely in the saddle, hands clutching tightly at the reins. With some measure of patience, Craig showed her the correct grip and tension, then adjusted the stirrups to a more suitable length for her legs.

'All set,' he said. 'Don't look so worried, we're not going to be doing anything but walk, initially.'

'Boring for you,' she commented apologetically. 'This could really have waited. You wanted a proper ride.'

'Which I'll have once we've given you twenty minutes or so. Long enough for your first time.' He gave the gelding a pat on the neck, then turned away to swing himself effortlessly up on the big chestnut. 'Use your knees to get him moving, not your heels. He's trained to respond to pressure rather than a kick in the ribs. And sit up straight!'

Jessica followed instructions as well as she was able, determined not to let him put her off. He was putting on the pressure deliberately, she was sure. So let him. She could take it. She would learn to control this animal if it killed her!

They rode down towards the lake, moving side by side at a slow pace. After a few minutes Jessica began to relax and enjoy the motion, her body automatically settling deeper into the saddle.

'That's better,' Craig observed without appearing to look her way. 'Now we can talk.'

'About what?' she asked, trying to sound as casual as he did.

'You, mostly. How are you settling in?'

'Fine.' She was wary of the question, for no obvious reason. 'I feel as if I've been here for weeks already.'

'Then shall we take it you have and dispense with this trial business,' he returned matter-of-factly. 'My mother is anxious for you to stay.'

'No more worries about Leo?' she couldn't resist asking, and saw his lips take on a slant.

'I'll always have problems where Leo's concerned, but I'm willing to accept that I could have been wrong about your interests.'

It was the nearest she was going to get to a full retraction, Jessica realised. 'I'm willing if you are,' she said. Tongue in cheek she added, 'Thank you, Mr Stafford.'

'I think we'd better make it Craig,' he returned on a dry note. 'Comfortable?'

'Oh yes.' Right then she would have said the same had every bone in her body ached. 'You must really regret being away from all this so much of the time.'

He shrugged. 'I'm not cut out to play the country gentleman. I prefer a less placid scene. It's nice to come home too, but I wouldn't want to stay.'

'You expect Leo to stay.' The words were out before she could stop them, drawn from her by some sharp and irrational sense of disappointment. 'He doesn't seem particularly cut out for it either.'

'Leo is cut out for nothing which includes work,' Craig responded on a harder note. 'You can't have been here for more than a week without discovering that for yourself. Supposing he left Morley, what kind of job do you think he'd be able to hold down?'

She had gone too far, Jessica decided, to back down now. 'I don't suppose he'd know himself until he'd tried one or two.'

'Working for whom?' He caught the quality in her silence and turned his head to look at her. 'You're not suggesting I should find him a job, by any chance?'

'It shouldn't be too difficult,' she said. 'There must be some kind of opening for him.'

'Except that I don't choose personnel, and I wouldn't expect those who do to do me any favours.'

'Afraid of being accused of nepotism?'

It was a moment or two before he answered that one. When he did it was on an odd inflection. 'You take a lot on yourself. One might almost think you had some personal involvement in the outcome.'

She was personally involved with every single member of this family, yet it was still impossible to say so. 'I apologise,' she said quickly. 'Of course it's none of my business. Do you think I'm ready to try a trot?'

Grey eyes glinted suddenly. 'Let's see, shall we?'

Dorian followed the chestnut into a change of pace without prompting. Lacking any notion of how to rise with the motion, Jessica found herself jolted unmercifully in the hard saddle and was hard put to keep her seat at all. It lasted bare moments, but it was more than enough. She clutched at the pommel as both horses came to a halt, hair tumbled about her face.

'That was the sitting trot,' Craig advised her with a hint of malice. 'You'd better get down for a few minutes before we start back and stretch your legs—no, not that way. Take both feet out of the stirrups and bring your right leg over, then just slide to the ground, then you don't run any risk of being dragged if the horse starts forward.'

He dismounted himself while he was telling her, taking Dorian's reins and looping both sets loosely over a convenient branch. 'We'll walk down to the water. It's just through the trees there.'

The lake looked placid in the afternoon sunlight, its surface scarcely ruffled by the slight breeze. Jessica picked up a pebble and attempted to skim it over the water, wrinkling her nose wryly when it sank with a single plop.

'I never could do that,' she said. 'I'm not even sure why I want to. Something to do with achievement, I suppose.'

'You're not keeping your throwing arm low enough,' Craig advised. He took another pebble himself and showed her, leaving a satisfactory wake of spreading ripples. 'Not exactly an essential accomplishment, but if it makes you happy——'

It took about five minutes for her to learn the correct technique. Success brought a sparkle to her eyes and a laugh to her lips.

'I know it's ridiculous,' she said, 'but I really feel I could conquer mountains at this moment! Thanks for the patience. I'm not a quick learner.'

Craig had been standing close behind her, the better to guide her arm into the right position. She stiffened a little but made no resistance when he turned her towards him, too well aware that she wanted what was about to happen. His mouth was exactly the way she had imagined it: firm and compelling. Response leapt in her, curving her body closer into the circle of his arms in involuntary surrender, moving her lips softly beneath his.

'Witch,' he murmured against the corner of her mouth. 'Green-eyed, red-haired witch! You knew I wouldn't be able to keep my hands off you if we got this close again. I've thought of little else this last week.'

'Nor I,' Jessica admitted unsteadily. 'It was so quick. One minute I was hating you, the next . . .'

'We both know what happened next.' He drew back a fraction to look at her, smile faint and reminiscent. 'More precisely, it happened the first time we met. Why else did you imagine I let you stay on? Why do you think I told you to stay clear of Leo? He's too young for you, anyway.'

'I know.' Her eyes searched his, uncertain of what she saw there. 'Craig . . .'

Mr Stafford!' Someone was calling from the path where they had left the horses tethered, half hidden by the trees. 'Phone call—urgent! They left a number to ring straight back.'

Craig swore softly beneath his breath and let Jessica go, waving a hand in acknowledgement.

'Not two minutes back in the country,' he growled. He looked down at her for a brief moment with a narrowed, almost calculating expression, then appeared to come to a decision. 'I'm going to have to get back in a hurry. I've a good idea what this will be about. If I put you on your horse do you think you can manage to come back slowly on your own? Dorian will take you if you give him his head. A horse returning to stables rarely makes any detours.'

'Of course,' she said with a certainty she didn't quite feel. 'I'll be fine.'

Watching him canter off a few minutes later, she found it difficult to believe that he was the same man who had kissed her so demandingly down by the lake. His touch just now had been so impersonal, his attention obviously elsewhere. Some business crisis, she imagined; certainly one he had been half expecting, from the sound of it. Any woman interested in such a man would have to learn to share him much of the time.

She was getting ahead of herself, she thought wryly at that point. He had kissed her once, that was all. He mightn't even have done that had he known the truth. Distant though the relationship was it made a difference. It had to make a difference. She only wished she had come here openly in the first place.

The groom was waiting to take her mount from her when she finally made it. Feeling a little stiff, she made her way into the house. Mrs Stafford was on her way downstairs. She stopped when she saw Jessica, her face expressing solicitous enquiry.

'Craig said he had to leave you to come back alone. I hope you didn't have any trouble?'

'None,' Jessica acknowledged. 'I just took it easy as he said, and the horse did the rest. Did he make his phone call?'

'Yes, he did.' The sigh was resigned. 'He's going back to town.'

'Now?'

'As soon as he's changed. And I was looking forward to having the whole family together at dinner for once.'

'I suppose,' Jessica said carefully, 'business has to take priority.'

'It does with Craig. Not that I can complain too

much—he's been the best kind of son in other ways.' Mrs Stafford looked up as the subject under discussion came along the gallery. 'You're going to have something to eat before you go, I hope.'

'I'll stop on the way,' he said. 'Sorry about this, but it's needs must.' He came on down the stairs, his glance flicking over Jessica without change of expression. 'Tell Beth to remember what we talked about on the plane.'

'You'll be back for the Ball, won't you?' his mother called after his fast departing figure. 'You have to be back for the Ball!'

'I don't know.' He didn't pause. 'I may have to fly out to the Middle East if this thing develops, so don't count on it.'

He was gone before any reply could be made to that. Not that any reply which could have been made would have altered matters, thought Jessica depressedly. With Craig gone the house seemed to have lost something vital—or was it just she who felt the emptiness?

'So that's that,' Mrs Stafford said flatly, echoing her thoughts. 'Come on down as soon as you're changed and we'll have a civilised cup of tea. At least some things can be relied upon!'

CHAPTER FIVE

THE rest of the weekend dragged, despite Jessica's efforts to fill it. She was thankful when Monday morning came round and she could occupy her mind with work again.

The news at tea-time that Craig was on his way to Saudi Arabia plummeted her spirits to rock bottom. There was scant chance now that he would make the Ball, and without him the affair held little attraction. Not that it made so much difference, she told herself in an attempt at consolation. On Saturday Caroline would be here. He might have spared her, Jessica, a couple of dances, but that would probably have been all. The things he had said to her down by the lake had been just words—the kind any man might use to a woman he found attractive. Had there been time and she had been willing he would no doubt have taken things further, and still thought nothing of it.

Her own emotions were far from clear. She had wanted him too; she still did—but was it simply physical? In many ways she hoped so. Falling in love with Craig would be futile, especially considering her secret. If he ever did find out about that he would throw her out of the house, she was sure of it. If only she had told the truth from the beginning.

'How is it that someone in Craig's position has to do so much running about?' she asked Mrs Stafford casually that evening when they were alone together. 'I'd have thought it was more an overseas contracts manager's job to do that for him.'

'Not with the Arabs, my dear. They expect the top man and feel slighted if they don't get him. In any case,

Craig prefers to handle the more important contracts himself. He never was one for sitting in an office.' She paused there. 'Talking of offices, has that other son of mine started pulling his weight yet?'

The simple answer to that was no, yet Jessica found it difficult to say. 'I don't think Leo is one for sitting in an office either,' she got out at length. 'He prefers the active side of the job.'

'Just so long as he makes some contribution. I'd hate him to finish up like Uncle Philip who never did a real day's work in his life.' She caught Jessica's startled glance and smiled. 'Yes, I know he's a charming old gentleman. That's what frightens me, because Leo is so much like him. The house belongs to Craig. Why should the woman he marries be expected to put up with three generations of relatives?'

'I imagine most would appreciate the situation,' said Jessica delicately. 'After all, the house is big enough.'

'I hope you're right. Not that marriage seems to be an imminent prospect.'

Jessica had to ask the question, trying to infuse a suitably casual inflection. 'What about Caroline Paige? I met her last week. She seemed a very suitable match.'

'Yes, there was a time when I thought it would be Caroline, but they never seem to get any further. Unless Craig is simply biding his time, of course, although at thirty-four he can't afford to do that much longer if he wants to enjoy his children. The trouble with Caroline is she's so independent. She wouldn't be prepared to stay home and wait for Craig to come back to her, and that's the kind of wife I fancy he'd want.'

'She could go with him,' Jessica pointed out, and received a shake of the greying head.

'Business trips are never very much fun for wives, from all I hear, and I shouldn't think he'd want the distraction. What he needs is a woman who will love him enough to wait until he has time for her, but I don't know where he's going to find one like that. Just take this time, for instance. A little more than a couple of hours at home and he's off again. What woman would put up with that?'

What woman indeed? Jessica thought, and closed her mind to the invading images.

The day of the Ball was cool and cloudy with little hope of improvement confining preparations indoors. Jessica's costume arrived around mid-morning, along with those for Craig and Leo. There had been no word from the former all week, which made the chances of his turning up in time remote. Jessica had schooled herself not to care, but knew it was only an act. Just to have Craig in the house would have made all the difference. Without him the whole event held no enticement.

Preparations went on apace during the afternoon, culminating in the arrival of the musicians at seven. The Long Gallery looked magnificent, the doors removed from the rooms opening off it to allow freedom of movement. Supper was to be a fork buffet served downstairs in the dining room. A hired staff would take care of the drinks and canapés.

Jessica's hair caused her a few problems, and she was still struggling with it at eight when the knock came on her door.

'Not ready yet?' asked Beth, putting her head round. 'What are you trying to do?'

'Attach this,' Jessica held up the cluster of ringlets. 'Only I can't seem to hide the base properly. Do you have time to give me a hand?'

'Of course. Nobody's arrived yet.' Beth came into the room, twirling for effect. 'How do you like it?'

She was dressed as a French maid in the shortest of black dresses, her long, slender legs encased in sheer black stockings that finished just about on a level with the dress hem, allowing tantalising glimpses of bare thighs and suspenders. A tiny frilly apron and froth of white lace on her pale red curls completed the outfit.

'Naughty but nice,' Jessica commented laughingly. 'You'll have the male element foaming at the mouth when they see the suspenders!'

'That's the idea.' Beth's giggle sounded very young. 'Helen suggested it—she said I had the legs for it. Now, let's see to your hair. How is it supposed to look?'

'The way Napoleon would have liked to see it,' Jessica responded wryly. 'I'm beginning to regret my choice of costume.'

'Oh no, you'll make a fabulous Josephine! Look, I'll set the piece up high like this so it falls down the back, then swathe your own hair over the base.' Deftly she suited her actions to words, standing back to admire the effect. 'Perfect! Put your dress on and we'll go down together. Mummy is going to throw a fit when she sees this outfit of mine. She'll want to know why I'm not wearing tights, for one thing.'

'I'm sure she'll have a very good idea why you're not wearing tights,' said Jessica, tongue in cheek. She took the blue dress out from its cover and slid down the long, concealed zip at the back in order to pull it on over her hips. 'Not exactly authentic for the period, but it certainly makes it easier to get into and out of. Will you zip me up again, please?'

Beth did so, looking over her shoulder to the reflection in the facing mirror with an unladylike little whistle. 'And you think *I'll* have the men foaming at the mouth! This is what I call a revelation.'

'Do you think it's too low?' asked Jessica anxiously, viewing the expanse of creamy skin exposed by the square neckline. 'I suppose I could always put a piece of lace or something across the front.'

'No way. Napoleon wouldn't have stood for it!' The grey eyes sparkled the way her brother's rarely did.

'We'll make a grand entrance, me all legs and you—well, it speaks for itself, doesn't it?' She grinned at Jessica's expression. 'Stop worrying, I'm only teasing. Believe me, there'll be others present far more scantily dressed than either of us. Last year a couple of Leo's invited guests turned up as artist and nude model. All she had was a long scarf what you might call "strategically draped". Mummy was wonderful. She just looked the girl straight in the eye and asked her if she didn't think it was cool for the time of year.'

'Good for her!' Jessica pulled on the long gloves that went with the outfit and adjusted the diamond and pearl choker about her throat—imitation, naturally, but surprisingly effective in appearance. The neckline still worried her, until she donned the black velvet mask and saw her identity disappear behind the winged eyepiece.

'Heavens, I forgot my mask!' Beth exclaimed, and went to fetch it, returning moments later with her own face similarly concealed. 'They've begun arriving,' she advised. 'Mummy is doing the receiving so there's no great rush. Did you invite anyone?'

'I don't know anyone,' Jessica denied. Something prompted her to add a rider to that. 'Except Doctor Turner, that is, but he already had an invitation.'

It was impossible to gauge Beth's reaction behind the mask. Even her voice sounded different. 'You know Peter?'

'Oh, we've met a couple of times,' Jessica was sorry now that she had mentioned the name. 'He seems a very nice person,'

'Yes, he is.' Beth's tone was a little abrupt. 'Shall we go down?'

Guests arrived thick and fast over the next half hour or so, and in a fascinating variety of costumes. There were duplications, of course, including at least three Harlequins and a couple of Robin Hoods, but none of them seemed in the least put out.

Jessica's own outfit drew some interest, especially from one magnificent Cavalier complete with curling beard and periwig. It took her several minutes to recognise Leo behind all the hair, and only then because she knew his laugh.

'I'd have come in a tricorne if I'd known,' he declared. 'We should be a pair, you and I. Come to think of it, I've seen a Napoleon somewhere, but he isn't nearly good enough for you. Did you dance yet?'

'Twice,' she acknowledged. 'Once with Charlie Chaplin and the other with Dracula. Beth seems to be having a good time.'

'A little too good, according to Mother. I've an idea she's trying to prove something to somebody.'

'Like Peter Turner, for instance? He did turn up, I suppose?'

'He's the Cossack,' Leo confided. 'Why don't you go and cheer him up a little? He tells me you two know each other. We'll have our dance later.'

There was only one Cossack and he seemed to have disappeared. Jessica ran him to earth eventually in the library seated in one of the big wing chairs with a whisky decanter at the side of him.

'I'm not on call,' he stated on a note halfway between defensiveness and belligerence before she could comment. 'I've a right to a drink if I feel like it!'

'Every right in the world,' she agreed. 'In fact I'll join you—unless you'd rather be alone?'

He shook his head, mood suddenly changing. 'Sorry, Jessica, that wasn't very polite of me. I'd like you to stay. What will you have?'

'Vodka and tonic if available,' she said, moving forward to take a seat as he rose from his. 'Gin if it isn't. I can't stand whisky.' She waited until he had poured the drink and brought it across before adding lightly, 'How did you know who I was right away?'

'You and Beth are the only ones here with hair that

colour,' he returned, 'and I know what she's wearing tonight.'

'You've spoken with her?'

'Not in any depth.' His smile was wry. 'It seems I was wrong about those lasting feelings. She made it plain she'd hardly thought about me while she'd been away.'

'I'm sorry.' There was little comfort Jessica could offer, but she attempted to lessen the sense of rejection a little. 'You know, she's really rather young for her age. Perhaps you stampeded her into the idea of marriage before she was ready for it. It doesn't mean she feels nothing for you.'

'It was Craig who did it,' Peter declared with an edge of bitterness. 'He thinks I'm not good enough for her. If my father had a title, or even a knighthood, I might have stood a chance.'

'Craig doesn't have a title,' she pointed out.

'No, but there's every chance he'll make the Honours lists in the next couple of years. Sir Craig Stafford—sounds good, doesn't it? He's hardly going to be content to see his sister as plain Mrs Turner.'

'I don't think he sees her making a very good doctor's wife,' Jessica defended. 'Ask yourself honestly, Peter, do you?'

The light of battle died suddenly from his eyes, his shoulders slumping. 'I suppose not. I could afford our own home, and someone to come in and clean, but nothing compared to what she's known all her life. That Swiss finishing school she went to only prepared her for life as a rich man's wife. I doubt if she can even boil an egg.'

'Perhaps you should find yourself a girl who can,' Jessica ventured.

'Yes, that would be sensible, wouldn't it?' He remained still for a moment looking into his glass, then made a visible effort to pull himself together. 'To hell with it! Let's go and join the party.'

Jessica left her own barely touched drink where it was; she hadn't really wanted it in the first place. Large as it was, the house appeared thronged with people. They had to push their way through a laughing crowd on the stairs. Plenty more were dancing. From where she stood, Jessica could see Leo holding Marie Antoinette in his arms. Caroline, she guessed, for no apparent reason except that it seemed the kind of costume a blonde would choose.

A tall Arab caught her eye as she took to the floor with Peter. He was standing by the main door apparently watching the dancers. His costume looked completely authentic. Had it not been for the mask hiding the upper part of his face above the neatly trimmed beard he could well have been the real thing.

She was surprised and a little disconcerted when Peter pulled her closer to lay his cheek against hers. Only when she saw the couple moving parallel with them did she realise what he was trying to do. To disengage herself from his embrace in front of Beth would hardly be good for his already dented pride, yet she didn't want to give others the wrong impression either.

In the end she waited several moments before gently pulling away, putting back her head to look him in the face. 'Don't use me to try and make Beth jealous,' she said, and softened the words with a smile. 'I have to live in the same house!'

'Sorry.' He looked a little abashed. 'I wasn't thinking. At least, I was, but about myself, not you. I'm not going to give up, not just like that. She was so sure about everything before she went away.'

'If she had been she wouldn't have gone,' Jessica felt bound to point out. 'Craig couldn't force her to leave— any more than he could force her to stay away from you now, even if he were here.'

'You talk too much sense,' Peter growled, 'even if it is

good for me. Can I call on you when I get low?'

'If you think I'll be any help.'

'Oh yes,' he said, 'you'll help. Just having someone to tell it to helps.'

People were starting to eat when they came off the floor. Jessica murmured some excuses about not being hungry yet when Peter offered to fetch a couple of plates.

'You go ahead,' she invited. 'I need to go and find Mrs Stafford in any case.' She gave him a bright smile. 'See you later!'

She was going to have to watch her step with Peter, she told herself ruefully as she moved away. There was a very real danger that he might latch on to her on the rebound; she had seen it happen on a couple of occasions with others. She liked him very much, but he did not attract her. There was only one man who could make her heart beat faster, and he wasn't here.

The Arab was still standing by the door when she reached it. Without appearing to move very fast, he was suddenly blocking her way, indicating the dance floor with an inclination of his head.

'Sorry,' she said, 'I'm looking for someone. Have you seen Mrs Stafford at all?'

'Not in the last half hour,' replied a voice she knew only too well. 'If she's running true to form she probably has her feet up where she isn't likely to be disturbed.'

'Craig?' Jessica could barely contain the eager response. 'I thought . . . When did you get back?'

'About an hour ago.'

'No one said anything.'

'No one knows what costume I'm wearing.' He paused, expression impossible to define behind the mask. 'Any particular reason you wanted my mother?'

She shook her head, hardly able to say she had been using her as an excuse to get away from Peter for a spell. 'I just wondered if there was anything needed doing, that's all.'

'I can't think what might. It all seems to be going well.' He took hold of her arm just above the elbow, his fingers firm through the silky material of her glove. 'Shall we have that dance?'

If Peter saw her dancing again after what she had just said he was going to have his ego flattened some more, Jessica realised, yet she couldn't find it in herself to refuse. Craig was here. She could still hardly believe it. The whole evening had taken on a totally different aspect.

This time there was no sense of disconcertion when she was drawn close, only a leaping pulse rate and a feeling of belonging. She wanted to say his name softly over and over again, to put her lips to his, beard and all. Foolish, of course, considering the way things were. Craig might find her physically good to be with too, but that was as far as it went.

'I think Miss Paige came as Marie Antoinette,' she told him, turning the screw a little deeper. 'She was dancing not so long ago.'

'I saw her.' There was no change of inflection. 'She's as easily recognisable as you are, though for different reasons. You and Beth stand out like a pair of beacons.' He paused. 'You seem to be on pretty close terms with Peter Turner. When did you meet?'

'The very first time I came to Harrogate,' she said, trying not to rush the telling. 'But I didn't realise he had any connection with Morley until after I took this job. It isn't really the way it looked. He . . .'

'It isn't important.' Craig sounded abrupt. 'Just so long as he leaves Beth alone.'

'I think she's already taken care of that herself.'

'So he turned to you for consolation. Well, I'm glad she's seen sense at last. Time enough to think about marriage when she's done some growing up.'

Jessica said carefully, 'She went to finishing school, didn't she? I always imagined they turned out a complete adult product.'

'No amount of schooling can change basic nature. She's still the same little tomboy underneath the gloss.' His tone altered suddenly. 'I'm sick of these damned masks. Let's go somewhere we can take them off.'

Jessica went because she couldn't have said no to save her life; because she wanted to be alone with him too. No one recognised him on their progress through the milling throng—or if they did they were saying nothing. She felt some faint constraint when she realised where they were headed, but made no comment until they were safely inside the room with a light switched on. Two rooms, in actual fact, she realised, looking about her, with the archway knocked into the dividing wall providing access from sitting to sleeping area. Unlike the rest of the house, the décor and furnishings in here were modern, though not aggressively so. The whole effect was one of deep rich comfort.

Craig removed his own mask first, then reached out a hand to do the same for her.

'That's better,' he said softly. 'Now I can see your face. The beard's stuck fast for the present, I'm afraid. Do you mind?'

'No.' Her voice was little more than a whisper. 'Craig, I . . .'

'Don't talk,' he said. 'I didn't bring you here to talk.'

He drew her to him, one hand sliding round the back of her neck beneath the fall of ringlets, the other tilting her chin. The beard felt real enough and not at all unpleasant, just lightly brushing her skin as he teased her lips apart. He deepened the kiss by slow degree, passing from playfulness to passion in a manner that had every sense in her rising to the occasion. A well-practised technique, she realised, yet she couldn't find it in herself to care. She was the one he was kissing right now, and that was all that mattered.

There was a long chesterfield sofa close by. He picked her up and laid her on it without taking his mouth away from hers, kneeling at the side of her to move his lips slowly and sensually down the line of her throat to the swelling curve of her breasts.

'You're magnificent,' he murmured against her skin. 'Lovely, lovely Jessica! God, but I want you!'

She wanted him too—there was no denying that. It was an ache inside her. She ran her fingers through the dark hair, feeling the shuddering deep down in her limbs, the heat rising from the very pit of her stomach. It would be so very easy to just give in to it, to let him carry her through to the big double bed and make total abandoned love. Only what about tomorrow, and the next day, and the one after that? Did she want an affair of the kind that involved sneaking around behind closed doors until Craig went away again?

'We'd better be getting back,' she whispered painfully, holding his head away from her. 'Before we're missed.'

'You're the only one who knows I'm here,' he said.

'Before I'm missed, then.'

Craig laughed softly, his hands moving to caress the flesh his mouth had so recently left. 'It's a big place, darling. You could be anywhere. Relax—forget about everybody else. There's just you and me, and we both want the same thing. Come on through to the bedroom. We'll be more comfortable out of all this gear.'

Jessica sat up slowly as he got to his feet and began to move away, obviously expecting her to follow. She felt the urge to do exactly that, but some stronger instinct pulled her back.

'You're taking too much for granted,' she got out. 'I'm sorry, Craig, but this is as far as it goes.'

He turned back to look at her, mouth thinning to a

harder line as he studied her face. 'Just like that?' he asked. 'A moment ago you were as ready as I was.'

'A moment ago I wasn't thinking straight,' she came back unsteadily. 'You have that effect on me. I—It's going too fast. You've kissed me just once before tonight.'

'And I wanted you then too, only circumstances didn't allow for it.' Craig made a sudden impatient gesture. 'Stop playing hard to get, Jessica. We're two adult people with similar needs. I think I can guarantee not to disappoint you.'

'I'm not playing hard to get.' She said it through her teeth, anger coming to her rescue. 'I don't doubt your experience for a moment, but I'm not going to add to it. I'm going back to the party.'

'Oh, no, you're not!' He was on her as she got to her feet, hands hard as iron on her arms as he swung her to face him. The grey eyes had a dangerous glitter. 'You've left it a little too late to start backing out.'

'It's never too late to change one's mind,' she denied, refusing to cower to his anger. 'I am *not* going to bed with you, Craig, and that's an end of it. Go and find yourself some other—victim!'

'You little bitch!' The words came out like a whiplash. 'You did that deliberately, didn't you?' His hands tightened on her as she looked at him mutely. '*Didn't* you?'

'Of course not.' She made a valiant attempt to pull away from him, desisting only when she realised he had no intention of letting her go. 'Craig, stop this! I've a right to turn you down if I want to. Every woman has that right.'

'Only if she's prepared to accept the consequences.' Eyes unrelenting, he let go one arm to reach behind her and yank down the long zip at the back of her dress, watching the bodice fall forward with a twisted smile. 'I'll at least see what I'm missing.'

She struggled wildly with him as he pulled the gown from her, but he was too strong for her. Clad only in the long waist slip and pearl choker, she stood there in front of him with breath coming raggedly, forcing herself not to make the move to cover her breasts with her hands in time-honoured fashion, head held high.

'So what now?' she asked contemptuously. 'Do you rip the rest off too?'

His expression had changed, the anger giving way to something less easily defined. For a long moment he made no move, then he stooped to pick up the discarded garment, holding it out to her. 'Get dressed and get out of here,' he said tightly, and turned his back on her.

Jessica drew on the costume with trembling fingers, managing the zip somehow. Craig was still standing looking into the empty fireplace when she finished, head bowed, hands thrust into the side splits of his robe.

'I'll leave first thing in the morning,' she said. 'And don't bother about salary. I'll put the last two weeks down to experience.'

He made no attempt to stop her leaving the room. She did so without haste, stifling the urge to cut and run. Not half an hour ago she had been in some kind of seventh heaven because Craig had come home; now she wished herself a million miles away from him. How could she have been such a fool as to hope that his interest in her might be anything but what it obviously was? He saw her only as something to be used.

There seemed more people than ever milling about the house. One or two, seeing her without her mask, thought it must be midnight already and took off their own. Jessica had almost reached the haven of her room when she met Mrs Stafford coming away from it. The older woman looked at her strangely, almost as if seeing her for the very first time.

'I just left something in your room,' she said. 'I'd rather you saw it on your own and then came down and talked to me about it. Will you do that?'

Realisation held Jessica transfixed for a moment. She knew. How there was no telling, but she knew!

'Of course,' she said quietly, fighting for the control to see things through to the bitter end. She was leaving anyway. Why should it matter any more? 'Where will you be?'

'In my room. I've just spent half an hour searching the attics, so I need to clean up a little.' Her gaze was very direct. 'I'll expect you in ten minutes.'

The portrait was the first thing Jessica saw on opening her door. It was propped on a chair facing her, dust still dulling the frame. She closed the door again and leaned on it to look at the painting, her breathing heavy as if she had been running.

It was a head and shoulders study of a young girl of perhaps eighteen or nineteen, her mass of bright hair swept up and away from her face to hang in a cluster of ringlets from crown to nape. Apart from the eyes she could have been looking at herself. The likeness was uncanny. Emma Stafford, condemned to the attics after her departure by a father who never forgave her. At some time Mrs Stafford must have seen this portrait and remembered it tonight when the similarity was at its most acute. Putting two and two together wouldn't have been difficult after that.

Drawn by some unseen force, Jessica moved across to view the painted features at closer quarters, putting out a tentative hand to touch the soft, full mouth. Her own felt bruised, her throat raw. Perhaps in some odd way she was paying for her grandmother's mistake.

The knock on the door made her start. Ten minutes, Mrs Stafford had said. Obviously she had changed her mind about waiting. She wanted the explanations now.

'Come in!' she called, and turned to meet her cousin,

breath catching in her throat when Craig opened the door. He was still wearing the full robe but was minus his mask, his face revealing a certain strain.

'Jessica ...' he began, then his eyes fell on the portrait at her side and he stopped abruptly, looking from it to her and back again in sudden narrowed concentration.

'Who the devil are you?' he demanded.

CHAPTER SIX

PRIDE came to Jessica's rescue, lifting her chin and steadying her voice. 'Meet your Great-Aunt Emma,' she said. 'She was my grandmother. That makes us cousins, Craig—three times removed, but still related. Devastating, isn't it?'

For a moment he made neither move nor reply, staring at her with eyes growing colder by the second. 'So why bring up the truth now?' he asked at last.

'I didn't, nor would I have done. Your mother brought me this. She's waiting for me to go and make my explanations in her rooms.'

'Then let's go,' he said. 'No point in you telling the same story twice.'

Jessica accompanied him without argument, aware that he had to know the whole thing some time. People looked at the pair of them oddly in passing, sensing the strain. It was Craig who knocked on his mother's door, Craig who opened it on her invitation to enter, ushering Jessica inside with a jerk of his head.

'I'm in on this too,' he said before his mother could speak. 'How long have you known?'

Louise Stafford looked from her son's coldly angry face to Jessica's white one and sighed. 'I only guessed tonight. As a matter of fact, it was Uncle Philip who opened my eyes. We were in the gallery when you came out of the library with Peter Turner. I think for a moment the shock took him back all those years. He even started to say the name Emma before he realised. That's when it came back to me. I used to enjoy browsing through the attics on wet days when I was younger. I remember finding the portrait and asking my husband who she was and why she wasn't downstairs with all the other family likenesses. Not on the stairs, of course, because that's reserved for the male heirs, but most of the Stafford women have been painted at some time in their lives, as you've probably noticed. Up until then I'd never even realised there had been an Emma Stafford. I wanted to set about tracing her, but he wouldn't hear of it. He thought it was best to leave well alone after all those years.' She paused, then added gently, 'Why didn't you tell us, Jessica? Surely we had a right to know?'

'I would have done eventually,' Jessica told her. Her voice sounded thick. 'I just wanted to—know you all a little first.'

'Size up the situation, you mean?' Craig's tone was harsh. 'Nice try, but it won't wash. You could have got to know us equally well by coming here openly in the first place.'

'As the poor relation?' she flashed. 'And what would you have thought about that? I didn't come to Morley because I wanted anything from the family, I did it because I had to know about my grandmother's background. For years I've wondered what kind of man would cast off his only daughter that way, but if he was anything like you I can well see it!'

'Craig does take after his grandfather in some ways,' put in Mrs Stafford before her son could speak, 'as his father did before him. But neither of them deserve the accusation you're making, Jessica.'

'She's entitled to her own opinion.' Craig's eyes were hard as agates, his jaw tense. 'You said something about leaving in the morning.'

'No!' Mrs Stafford's cry startled them both. She looked distressed. 'I want her to stay.'

'I can't stay.' It was Jessica's turn to be gentle now. 'I'm sorry it had to turn out like this. I didn't think far enough ahead. Forgive me.'

Neither mother nor son attempted to stop her from leaving. She felt close to tears but refused to give way. The deception was over; her secret out. And she wasn't wanted; Craig had made that painfully clear.

The revelries were still going strong, but the last thing she felt like was putting on a party face. Reaching her own room, she locked the door against any accidental intrusion and stood for a moment to collect herself. The portrait still sat where Mrs Stafford had left it, an accusation in itself. She should have known better, Jessica thought numbly. Her plan had been doomed to failure from the start. She was no longer even sure what she had hoped to gain from it.

She forced herself to move eventually, crossing to the closet to take out her suitcase and open it up on the bed. If she packed now she could be away first thing in the morning before anyone else was up and around. Better a quick, clean break than having to explain to Leo and Beth. No doubt Craig would do that for her.

Craig. The very thought of him made her curl up inside. So she wouldn't think about him, not now or any other time. Once she left Morley it was going to be as if these last couple of weeks had never happened.

The knock on the door went unheeded the first time. Only when it was repeated a little more insistently did she pause in her movements and look up, pulses jerking.

'Jessica.' The voice wasn't loud, but it was recognisable even through the thickness of the door. 'I know you're in there. I want to see you.'

Jessica knew what he wanted to say: all the things he had been unable to say in front of his mother. With the door securely locked she could always ignore him, but it wasn't in her to turn away from a confrontation.

Craig was standing with a hand resting against the jamb when she opened up, his face set hard. 'This isn't my idea either,' he said, 'so it's to be hoped we're both capable of compromise. Do I get to come in?'

'Of course.' She stood back to allow him entry, expression as cold as his. 'It's your house. If the morning isn't soon enough for me to leave I can always go tonight. I have my own transport.'

His gaze flickered over the half packed case on the bed before he turned to look at her. 'Mother wants you to stay,' he said. 'There are very few things she asks for, and I'd never willingly deny her. She's apparently become very fond of you while you've been here, and found you excellent company.' The last with a faint curl of the lip. 'For her sake, I'm inviting you to stay.'

'For her sake, I wish I could,' Jessica retorted, 'but I doubt if it's what you really want.'

'What I want isn't important. Not in this instance.' He paused, mouth hardening afresh at her lack of response. 'There's something else you should know. My mother has a heart condition—no, not a killing one,' he added as she drew in a sudden shocked breath. 'At least, not immediately. The chances are, however, that she won't live to see a ripe old age. That's why I'm keen that the life she does have is as full and happy as I can make it. If having our new-found cousin around gives her any kind of pleasure then I'm willing to go along. Naturally someone else would be found to take over your job.'

'No.' Jessica faced up to him resolutely. 'If I stay—and I only say *if*—it has to be on the same footing. I'd earn my keep—the way Leo does.'

'The day Leo does that will be the first.' He lifted his shoulders. 'Far be it from me to deprive the estate of your services. Just tell me—yes or no?'

He had left her no real choice. Not under the circumstances. She steeled herself to make it. 'Yes.'

There was no visible reaction. 'In that case we'd better get back to the party. It wouldn't do to have anyone think we'd gone to bed as early as this.'

Jessica flushed, remembering those moments in his room. 'You asked for that.'

'True,' he agreed disconcertingly. 'You played that little scene beautifully. I even came after you to apologise for having you wrong, until I found out what kind of a liar you really were.'

'I was lying by omission, that's all,' she denied. 'Everything else I've told you has been the truth.'

'I'm sure.' He sounded suddenly weary. 'You realise we're going to have to put on something of an act between us when my mother is around? She isn't going to be too happy if she realises the way things are. Still, I'm sure you can cope with a little more play-acting, starting right now. I said I'd take you back to her as soon as I'd straightened things out.'

They would never be that, Jessica thought desolately. Not now. She and Craig were light years apart.

Mrs Stafford was still in her room. She looked relieved to see the two of them together.

'I was afraid my silly little ploy with the portrait might have been taken the wrong way,' she confessed. 'At the time it seemed easier to do it that way than blurt it right out.'

'It would have been,' Craig assured her before Jessica could speak. 'It wasn't your fault that I saw it too and got a shock.' His smile made light of the following statement. 'I've made suitable amends for my initial reaction and she's agreed to stay on.'

'Oh, I'm so glad!' Mrs Stafford held out her hands to Jessica, drawing her forward to kiss her cheek. 'We're cousins too, you realise, despite the difference in our ages. You'd better start calling me Louise. My dear, there's so much I want to ask you, only not tonight. Go on back and enjoy the party.'

'I'd rather stay and talk to you, if you're not too tired,' Jessica admitted truthfully, avoiding Craig's eyes.

'No, I'm not. Well, if you're sure.' It was apparent

that this was what Louise herself really wanted. 'Craig, you should get back to our guests—I don't imagine Leo will be taking his duties as host too seriously. Come and sit down over here, Jessica. You told me last week that the only relatives you had left were very distant ones on your mother's side. Obviously that's us. But what about your father's family? Did he have no brothers or sisters either?'

'A brother,' Jessica admitted, relaxing to some extent with Craig gone from the room. 'He emigrated to Australia when I was about four, and I don't remember him at all.'

'You don't have any communication?'

'A card at Christmas—occasionally a letter.' She refrained from adding that she had kept up a regular correspondence herself for almost a year after her parents' deaths until finally discouraged by the obvious lack of interest. 'He married, but they don't have any children of their own. I rather gathered they never wanted any.'

'It takes all kinds.' The other woman's gaze was shrewd. 'Would you have gone even if you'd been asked?'

Jessica shook her head. 'At least I had friends here in England. They got me through the worst part.'

'You should have come to us then. Why didn't you?'

'I didn't have the courage. I'd only found out about Grandmother's past a few months before when Mum decided to tell me the story—perhaps she had some kind of premonition. Anyway, there was enough money for me to finish my course at business training college and see me through until I was earning a decent salary, so I wasn't in any dire need.'

'It wasn't money I was talking about. We would have welcomed you with open arms.' Louise smiled faintly at Jessica's look of doubt. 'Yes, even Craig. He might have thought Emma foolish for doing what she did, but he would never have cut her off in his grandfather's shoes. If he appeared less than overjoyed a little while ago when he first realised who you were it was only because he'd been taken unawares.'

'I should have told Leo who I was that very first time I was here,' Jessica admitted. 'But that offer of a job was such a temptation. You see, even if you'd welcomed me with open arms, as you put it, I'd never have been sure whether you were doing it out of a sense of duty. At least this way I know you want me to stay for myself.'

'Very much so. I've enjoyed this last couple of weeks far too much to countenance doing without you. They must find someone else to take over your job, of course. You're one of the family now.'

'I'd rather keep it,' Jessica responded. 'I've already told Craig that.'

'And he agreed?'

There was only one answer she could make. 'Yes, he agreed. It's hardly arduous work, and the hours leave me plenty of free time.'

'Well, if it's really what you want.' Louise was obviously a shade disappointed. 'I'd hoped we would be able to take some drives together—perhaps to the coast. I haven't been to the coast for several years.'

'We can do it at the weekend,' promised Jessica. 'I'd enjoy that too. Grandmother told me about a place called Whitby. It used to be her favourite spot when she was a child, she said.'

'You knew she was from Yorkshire, then?'

'Yes. She just never went into any detail. I can't say I thought much about it. I wasn't at an age then to think deeply about anything very much.'

'So you were only young when Emma died?'

'About eleven. She only outlived Grandfather by a few months. I don't think she wanted to live without him.'

'It's possible. They must have been very much in love to start with, and it doesn't always fade with time.' Louise was silent for a moment, eyes introspective as if remembering something from her own past life, then she seemed to give herself a mental shake, looking up with a smile on her lips. 'I suppose there's a lot we'll never know, but at least we can make some amends. Uncle Philip will be delighted. He was just a boy when Emma left, but he told me once that home was never the same afterwards. They were all of them forbidden to even speak of her—a very hard man, was Craig's grandfather. Where business is concerned Craig is perhaps the same, only don't let that side of him blind you to everything else. I know I'm his mother and obviously biased, but he's worth getting to know properly before passing any final judgments.'

'I know he'd do anything to please you,' Jessica returned steadily, 'and that impresses me a great deal. Don't worry, we'll find a level.'

'I certainly hope so.' Louise smiled and patted her hand. 'And now I'm going to insist that you go back to the party. We have plenty of time to talk.'

Jessica rose with reluctance. 'You won't come out again yourself?'

'No, my dear, I've had enough. Things usually start hotting up—as Leo would put it—once the masks come off, and these days I can't quite take the pace. You go and enjoy yourself. I'll see you in the morning.'

The party certainly was hotting up, Jessica acknowledged moments later, threading her way through the laughing revel-makers who seemed to be everywhere. The fact that everyone appeared to know everyone else made her feel very much the odd man out. She was heartily glad to see Peter approaching, his Cossack's hat rakishly askew.

'Been looking for you everywhere,' he shouted above

the din of voices and music. 'Haven't you eaten yet? There's plenty left.'

'I'm not hungry,' she denied. 'I was on my way downstairs to get some fresh air.'

'Good idea, I'll join you.' He took her hand to draw her in the direction of the staircase, jerking his head in mock alarm as a conga line came swirling out of a doorway right across his line of advance. 'Hey, you lot, watch who you're mowing down!'

They were not so much mown down as picked up, hands reaching out to drag them into line regardless of will or whim. Held firmly by a six-foot cowboy, Jessica gave in and entered into the spirit of the thing with abandonment. Enjoy the party, Louise had said. Very well, she would do just that. Time enough tomorrow to think about other matters.

She lost track of Peter after that, whirled away to dance by the cowboy when the line finally collapsed through loss of interest. Her new partner ran a stud farm some twenty miles away, she discovered over the next twenty minutes or so. Craig's chestnut had come from there.

'Bred by my father, not me,' he admitted. 'I've only just taken over the reins.' He laughed immoderately at the weak pun, sobering to add, 'You must get Craig to bring you over some time. In fact, I'll suggest it to him myself. How long are you staying at Morley?'

'I'm not sure,' Jessica said with caution. 'As long as I'm needed, I suppose.'

'Or until you get married,' he rejoined. 'Pretty girl like you shouldn't have to wait long.'

'That's reassuring.' The irony was mild. This male egotist believed he was paying her a genuine compliment. Why disillusion him?

She made her escape as soon as she was able, wondering whether to creep away to bed while the going was good. The sight of Arab robes closely enmeshed with pale blue crinoline skirts gave her further reason to wish herself elsewhere. Not for Caroline the ignominy of a quick proposition in a bedroom. She was his equal, to be treated with respect.

Peter caught up with her at just the right psychological moment. Here was a man who needed solace too. Why shouldn't they find it together? The smile she turned on him was warm in its welcome, the hand she put on his sleeve almost a caress. 'I thought you'd deserted me.'

'Never.' He was smiling too, his own hurt soothed by the quality of her greeting. 'Let's dance.'

This time Jessica made no demur when he drew her close, needing the comfort as much as he did. They were each using the other, which made it a fair exchange. For the first time in hours she felt the tension start to ebb.

She told him the truth of her background later over a drink in a quiet corner, wryly acknowledging her mistakes.

'I should have had the courage to tell them from the start,' she admitted. 'This way it has to look as if I had an ulterior motive, I suppose.'

'Only Craig would see it that way,' Peter responded. 'I understand why you did it.'

'I think Mrs Stafford does too,' Jessica smiled a little. 'I mean Louise. It's going to be difficult to remember to call her that.' She changed the subject then. 'You said your mother was away that very first time we met. Has she got back yet?'

'Heavens, yes. She only went for a week to visit her sister in Retford. That's about as long as Dad and I can manage without her to keep us organised. A G.P. needs a woman behind him more than most.' He paused. 'I'd like you to come and meet them, Jessica.'

She said quietly, 'Do they know about Beth?'

'Yes, but they never approved, so they're not going to be sorry it's over. You'll just be a friend—I'll make sure they both appreciate that fact. Let's make it tomorrow for tea. Sunday is a good day—unless there's an unexpected call.'

It was sooner than seemed wise, but she knew why he was doing it. It would take her mind off things too. 'Thanks,' she said. 'That sounds a nice idea. You'd better write down your address, then I can drive myself over. What time?'

'Oh, fiveish. Mum is Yorkshire born and bred. It's a roast and Yorkshire pudding for Sunday lunch whatever the weather, and high tea at six. Not that Dad would have it any other way. He enjoys his food.' He stirred with reluctance. 'People are starting to leave. I think it's time I went too. Don't forget, will you?'

'Of course not.' Jessica came to her feet along with him, sliding an arm companionably through his. 'I'll see you to the door.'

Craig was already in the hall, head bared beneath the glittering crystal chandelier, as he said goodbye to departing guests. There was no sign of either Beth or Leo, but Caroline stood at his side, completely at ease in her surrogate position.

Jessica waited over by the open doors while Peter paid his dues, fully aware that Craig had seen her and caring not one whit. She was tired, and intended making for bed as soon as Peter had gone, regardless of the fact that the party still appeared to be going strong for most. So much had happened tonight, and none of it as she had planned. She should have asked for time to consider whether or not she wanted to stay on— except that Louise's wishes deserved priority over her own. The other had shown her nothing but kindness since her arrival at Morley. To stay at her request was surely a small enough return.

She accompanied Peter to his car when he was ready, grateful that he made no attempt to kiss her goodnight before getting behind the wheel.

'Tomorrow,' he reminded her at the wound-down window. 'And thanks, Jessica. I don't know what I'd have done without you tonight. You helped me salvage my pride, if nothing else.'

And you mine, she thought, but refrained from saying it. No one else would ever know what had taken place between her and Craig. The memory alone was enough to bear.

On impulse she made her way across to the stables when Peter was gone, pausing at the half open door of the first box to say the gelding's name softly. He came at once, pushing his head at her with a little whickering sound of recognition, pleased to have company. Jessica had ridden several times during the past week under Beth's guidance, and hugely enjoyed the experience. She wished it were only possible to saddle up right now and take off on her own across the moonlit countryside. Facing the family wasn't going to be easy come the morning. There would be so many questions to answer, so many explanations to make. But face it she had to; she had given her word.

She returned to the house via the rear premises, thankful to find Craig gone from the hall. Things were beginning to quieten down at last, with small groups of people sitting around talking together in the manner of those too pleasantly exhausted to think of moving again for the present. Coffee was being served to those who wanted it—a sure sign that the end was in sight. Most of those still here would be staying the night, Jessica guessed. Judging by the look of some, it was a good thing too. At least they would have time and opportunity to sober up before taking to the road.

Leo appeared out of nowhere as she made her way across to the stairs, blocking her line of progress. He looked a little the worse for wear himself, wig askew, face flushed.

'We never had that dance,' he claimed. 'I demand compensation!'

'The party's over,' Jessica protested mildly. 'The musicians must be ready to pack up by now.'

'Not while there's anybody left up there to dance, and there is.' He slung a familiar arm about her shoulders, more, she felt, to steady himself than from any other motive. 'Never say die while there's life left in the old body! One dance won't kill you.'

Jessica didn't imagine it would, tired as she was. Easier anyway to just give in and get it over. 'Five minutes,' she said firmly, 'then I'm going to bed.'

'An even better idea. We'll go together.' He sobered suddenly and unexpectedly, looking down at her with a sheepish expression. 'Sorry, Jess, I've had too much to drink. Just forget I said that.'

'It's forgotten.' She gave him a swift, searching glance, taking in the change in him now he had relinquished the role of happy inebriate. 'You don't really want to dance, do you?'

He shook his head, arm dropping away from her. 'To be honest, I think you're right about the combo. They are packing up. It's gone three.' He signalled to the passing waiter, taking two cups of the ready-poured coffee and handing one of them to Jessica. 'We may as well sit right here on the stairs. I don't feel like mingling any more.'

He had done more than his fair share of it, Jessica mentally agreed, recalling the many different partners she had seen him with that night. Seeking solace, she had found herself thinking at one point, but from what she hadn't been sure.

'I didn't see your little friend from Skipton here tonight,' she remarked casually after a moment or two.

'I didn't invite her.' His tone was gruff. 'I took your advice and stopped seeing her. You were right, it wasn't fair to lead her on into thinking there might be something going for us. She's too sweet a kid to be used as a substitute.'

'For whom?' Jessica asked softly, sensing his need to confide. 'Caroline?'

He went very still. 'How did you know?'

Jessica couldn't honestly have said. The name had just come to mind. 'I suppose it must be a combination of things,' she admitted at length. 'Nothing conscious, just a series of impressions. Something in your voice when you say her name—the way you pretended to forget the night she was coming over to dinner. Does she know how you feel about her?'

'I try not to let her know. We're the same age, you see, and she prefers older men. She told me that much over a year ago, just before she and Craig started seeing each other on a regular basis.' He smiled a little. 'Strange, isn't it, how you can know someone all your life and then suddenly see them in a totally different way? I can remember the exact moment it happened. I'd taken my mother over to dinner at Thurlmere one night when Craig was away, and we got talking, just the two of us. Nothing special, only I suddenly realised that Caroline was the only girl I'd ever been able to talk to properly without being flip. I just looked at her sitting there smiling at me and I knew she was the only girl for me. Only for her nothing changed. I was and still am the boy she grew up with. Craig was in another league when we were in our teens.'

Unrequited love was almost a disease round here, thought Jessica wryly. First Peter and now Leo—with Craig an intruding factor in both cases.

'You may have the wrong idea about their relationship,' she ventured. 'If they were in love they'd surely have done something about it by now.'

'Like marriage, for instance? I don't think Caroline would be prepared to pay the price. That still doesn't do me any good.'

'It might if you gave her some indication.'

'No chance.' His tone was flat. 'Even if there is a way, what do I have to offer a girl like Caroline?'

'You'll be estate manager when Bob retires,' Jessica pointed out.

'Which won't be for another six years at least, unless Craig forces the issue. Anyway, I don't want to spend the rest of my life stuck here at Morley. I'm twenty-four now. Before I reach twenty-five I have to sort myself out. Do you think you'll stick it long enough to see me do it?'

'I'm not sure,' she admitted. 'Circumstances have altered.' She paused before continuing, already weary of explanations. 'Leo, there's something you have to know. I came here under false pretences.'

'You mean you really were after the silver?'

She smiled at the weak joke. 'I think your brother believes I had my sights set on something rather more subtle than a quick snatch. I imagine you've already heard the story of your Great-Aunt Emma?'

'Well, yes, she ran away with the chauffeur's son. What does——' He broke off, looking at her with sudden dawning enlightenment. 'Don't tell me you're something to do with her!'

'Her granddaughter,' Jessica admitted.

'Which makes us cousins, doesn't it?' Leo sounded genuinely delighted. 'Hey, that's great! I always knew there was something about you!'

Like mother like son, thought Jessica with gratitude. At least she could be sure of her welcome where these two were concerned. 'Don't you want to know why I wasn't open about it from the first?' she asked.

'I can guess why. You'd have wanted to be sure what kind of people you were claiming as family before you got involved.' His grin was almost as jaunty as of old. 'I take it we've passed muster. Am I the first to be given the news?'

'Not exactly,' she confessed. 'Your mother guessed. Apparently I look a lot like Emma did at my age—especially tonight.'

'No wonder she drove the chauffeur's son wild!'

'Idiot!' Jessica put an affectionate hand alongside his cheek for an instant. 'But nice with it.'

It was then as she took her hand away that she found her gaze going beyond him, drawn by some irresistible force. Craig stood just within the drawing room doorway watching them, face as hard as iron. Seen from that distance the gesture could easily have been misconstrued. Well, too bad. If she was going to stay here at all it was going to be on her terms not his.

Caroline came up behind him, putting a hand on his arm to say something which brought a softening of the tense features. He nodded and turned back into the room along with her, disappearing from sight.

'I really must get to bed,' said Jessica with flat intonation, 'or I'm going to be useless tomorrow. It isn't required that I stay till the bitter end, is it?'

'I don't see why you should.' Leo got up with her, taking the empty cup from her hand. 'I'll see to these. And don't worry about the morning, I doubt if anybody is going to be around much before lunchtime.' His smile warmed her. 'Night, Cousin Jess. I'm really glad you're here.'

Which was more than she could say for herself, she thought hollowly, making her escape. There was too much that hurt.

CHAPTER SEVEN

DESPITE her tiredness, it was gone five before she finally slept, awakening at eight-thirty feeling unrefreshed and more than a little depressed.

She could hear voices in the dining room when she went down. Pauline was just coming out of the door carrying a tray. Om impulse, Jessica asked if she could have coffee served out on the terrace, and went out into the morning sun, relieved to find she had the scene to herself. The last thing she felt like was company.

The lake sparkled in front of her, its surface undisturbed by even the merest hint of a breeze. It was too still and too hot for the time of day, Jessica thought. It could be that they were in for a storm later on. The rise in pressure could account for her depression, although she doubted if it were wholly responsible. Nothing was working out the way she had planned. The unmasking had come too soon.

Memory of Craig's treatment of her last night brought a tremor of distaste. He had been so arrogant, so utterly convinced that she would be ready to fall into his arms—and his bed—the moment he gave the word. Was there something about her that suggested an easy conquest? she wondered. Certainly her response to that first kiss a week ago had not been exactly reticent, but was that reason enough to assume what he had assumed?

The placing of the tray on the table at her elbow took her by surprise because she had not heard any footsteps. She turned her head to thank the maid, freezing into immobility when she saw Craig looking down at her. He was wearing a towelling robe and had a separate towel slung around his neck. His regard was anything but friendly.

'Don't you think the staff have enough to do today without catering for special orders?' he demanded.

Jessica flushed, aware that he had a point. 'I didn't think,' she confessed. 'I'd have fetched it myself except that Cook doesn't like anyone in her kitchen who isn't supposed to be there. Anyway, thank you,' she finished lamely.

'Don't mention it.' There was no softening of attitude. 'Just don't try taking advantage of your position, that's all.'

'That's unfair!' she exclaimed with heat, coming upright in the chair. 'You've no right to think . . .'

'I've every right,' he cut in. 'You manipulate Leo into giving you the job in the first place, make yourself indispensable to my mother, even—damn it—start working your way under my skin, then expect me to believe you'd no ulterior motive in coming here?'

The anger drained from her suddenly, leaving her flat and empty. She said tonelessly, 'I won't argue with you, Craig. Believe what you want.'

'I'll do just that.' There was a pause, brief but pregnant, before he added with deadly softness, 'Talking of relationships, we have some unfinished business to take care of. And we are going to finish it, believe *me*. I'm going to be around for a while taking that holiday Mother keeps telling me I need. Before it's over you and I are going to know one another a great deal better than we do now—*cousin*!'

Jessica bit her lip as she watched him walk away, aware that he wasn't joking. She had made a fool of him twice in his estimation, and while his hands were tied in one direction he was not a man to forget or forgive easily. Making her give in to him would be one way of equalling the score. And he could do it if he set his mind to it; she had few doubts on that score. Only he wasn't going to get the opportunity. From now on she would make sure she was never alone with him.

With several of last night's guests still lingering, lunch proved a somewhat noisy affair. Louise stayed in her rooms, sending down a request for Jessica to visit her there. Jessica found her up and dressed but obviously disinclined towards the effort of dissimulation with the people downstairs.

'We always get some who overstay their welcome,' she observed, inviting Jessica to a seat on the chair facing her own chaise-longue. 'Anyway, there's a good film on TV this afternoon. Do you like old movies?'

'Some of them,' Jessica admitted, and hesitated, aware of the implication. 'I'll be going out later. Peter Turner's invited me over to tea.'

There was a momentary silence. Louise looked disturbed. 'Does Beth know?'

'I don't think so.' Jessica looked her cousin straight in the eye. 'Do you think I should tell her?'

'Do you?' Louise countered.

'I don't know that she merits it. She gave the distinct impression last night that nothing Peter did was her particular concern any longer. Which is the only reason he turned to me. There's nothing more to it.'

'If there was you could neither of you be blamed.' Louise's voice was wry. 'Beth should have had the courage to face Peter with the truth.'

'Providing she knows what the truth really is. Personally, I think she still feels the same way about him, only . . .'

'Only Craig has planted doubts in her mind and she's confused.' Louise shook her head. 'He was right to pull her up. She had her head completely in the clouds where Peter was concerned. She isn't cut out to be a doctor's wife.'

'Maybe not right now,' said Jessica, 'but in a couple of years' time it could be a different story. He'd wait,

I'm sure of it. He'd wait any length of time if only he believed there was a chance. He really does love her, you know.'

'I'm sure he does. It's just . . .' Louise stopped and sighed. 'What I'm really trying to say is I doubt if my daughter will ever have the temperament to adjust to a whole new life style. She's been over-indulged by all of us.'

'But not spoiled. That's the important thing.'

'I'm glad you think not.' This time the pause was longer. When Louise spoke again it was with an entirely different inflection. 'Did Craig tell you he plans to take a holiday from business affairs for a while?'

'He mentioned it.' Jessica was hard put not to reveal any trace of satire in her voice. 'It will be nice for you to have him here.'

'Nice for us all. The whole house has a different feel to it when Craig is home.' Louise smiled suddenly. 'You know, Jessica, your coming here like this could be just what was needed. Old blood, but new too, if you see what I mean. I hope you and Craig can become friends.'

What she hoped was already becoming too transparently clear. Jessica hardly knew what to say in return. Close they would become if Craig had anything to do with it, but his intentions had little to do with what his mother was talking about.

'I'm sure we will,' she managed with reasonable conviction.

She stayed in her own room until it was time to leave for Harrogate around four, reluctant to run into any of the family. Leo was on the point of getting out of the Ferrari when she went outside. He paused when he saw her coming, taking in the bandbox-fresh white button-through dress with a lift of his brows.

'All dressed up in your Sunday best? What's the occasion?'

'I'm going out to tea,' she said, acknowledging the futility of trying to keep her destination secret. 'Just a friendly gesture on Peter's part.'

'I'm sure.' He added softly, 'I don't think Beth's going to like it much.'

'Perhaps that was part of his reason for asking me,' Jessica returned. 'I meant what I said, Leo. It's just a friendly visit.'

'I believe you. I doubt if Peter's your type either.' The blue eyes held a bland expression. 'Does Craig know you're going?'

'Nothing I do outside of working hours has anything to do with Craig,' she defended, getting behind the wheel of her own vehicle.

'Can I tell him that if he asks?'

'If you like.' She kept her tone indifferent. 'There's no particular reason for him to show any interest.' Giving him a fleeting smile, she closed the door and lifted a hand in farewell before switching on the ignition. For the next few hours she was going to forget all about Craig Stafford, she promised herself with determination.

Peter's home was a large detached on one of the quiet back streets, the surgery a sizeable extension to one side. Both Doctor and Mrs Turner she liked on sight, although she sensed a certain reticence in their welcome of her during those first moments of meeting. Peter's mother was far removed from the coolly collected and efficient medic's wife Jessica had more than half anticipated. Small and slight of build, she looked as if she had spent her life being cossetted by her menfolk rather than the other way round.

Tea proved to be a meal of such gigantic proportions Jessica felt over-faced before she even started. She did, however, manage to put away a creditable amount of the cold meats and salad, together with a helping of a home-made trifle too delicious to turn down. Both

Peter and his father ate enough for a small army to live on, causing her to wonder how they both managed to keep their weight down.

'Nervous energy,' advised Mrs Turner when she jokingly made the point while the two of them were clearing the table after the meal was over. 'They burn up all they eat between them. You know, as a guest, you should be sitting down and taking it easy, not doing this.'

'I'd rather help, if you don't mind,' said Jessica. 'If I go through and sit with Peter and his father they'll feel bound to talk about something I might be interested in, whereas I have the feeling they really want to discuss that case Doctor Turner mentioned.'

'You're probably right at that. Sometimes one of them can come up with something the other hadn't thought of just by talking it through.' The other woman looked at her. 'You're a very considerate young woman, Jessica. I can see why Peter is so taken with you.'

'There's nothing between us,' Jessica stated honestly, feeling she should make that much clear. 'We're friends, that's all.'

'Does Peter feel that way too?'

'Yes, he does.'

'Meaning he's still hankering after young Beth,' came the shrewd observation. 'I thought it was odd if he'd changed his mind so quickly. Only yesterday he was happy as a hunter because he was going to see her again. I tried to talk him out of it, considering she'd made no attempt to get in touch with him since she came home, but he wouldn't listen. Today he won't even mention her name. You were at the ball last night. Did he and Beth talk at all?'

'Not for long,' Jessica was bound to admit. 'I'm afraid Beth had something of a change of heart while she was away.'

'Hardly surprising. She's barely old enough to know her own mind. Craig did the best thing sending her away. The way things were with her and Peter it was impossible to talk sense into either of them—and heaven knows, both his father and I tried hard enough!'

'You mean because Beth isn't the type of girl to make a good doctor's wife?' ventured Jessica, reluctant to appear too inquisitive.

Mrs Turner shook her head. 'There's more to it than that. Beth is young for her age. She can't possibly know what she does want. I'm willing to believe she thinks— or at least thought—a lot of Peter, but she's nowhere near ready for marriage at all, much less to him. If they'd been willing to wait a couple of years it might have been different. Still, if Beth has changed her mind altogether it's probably for the best.' She lifted the tray she had been stacking and turned towards the door. 'If you'd like to bring those others through I'll get them in the dishwasher.'

Peter and his father were still deep in conversation when the two women went through to the sitting room, breaking off with some apparent reluctance to greet the newcomers.

'You'll have to forgive us,' Dr Turner appealed smilingly to Jessica. 'I needed a fresh outlook on this particular case. Doctors are terrible people for talking shop!'

'Only when they're together,' said his wife comfortably. 'Peter, why don't you take Jessica round the garden? It's looking at its best this time of year, and it's such a lovely evening.'

Her son turned a resigned face in Jessica's direction. 'That's another way of telling me I've been neglecting my guest! How about it?'

'I'd love to see the garden,' she said, tongue in cheek. 'A pity it wasn't as warm as this last night. We could have had dancing on the lawns.'

'With the groundsmen having fits this morning.' Smiling, he came to his feet. 'Come on then, let's take the tour. Not quite up to Morley standards perhaps, but Mum has green fingers with anything that grows.'

Jessica saw what he meant when they got outside. Although not large, the garden was beautifully planned and planted, the beds a riot of colour, the lawns like bowling greens. There was a little round summerhouse at the far end of the rose arbour, its sides latticed to let in light and air. Sitting there, Jessica breathed in the scent of roses and night-scented stock, letting the peace wrap around her.

'They like you,' Peter commented after several moments had passed in silence. 'Dad thinks you're the kind of girl a man should look for if he's considering settling down.'

Jessica didn't look at him. 'I hope you told him there was nothing like that between us.'

'Yes, I did. I'm not sure he accepted it.' The sigh came hard. 'They've both been pretty concerned about my feelings for Beth. I suppose another girl would be the obvious solution.'

'Only if she was one who could take Beth's place, and I'm not cut out for that.' She glanced at him then, a swift assessing glance. 'Be honest, Peter. You're not really attracted to me as a person.'

He smiled at that, one hand coming out to briefly cover hers. 'I like you tremendously.'

'The same way I like you. Only that's it, isn't it? We're two people who happen to get along rather well.'

'I suppose you're right. Nothing works out the way it should. I want Beth still and you . . .' he paused there, studying her enquiringly . . . 'what do *you* want, Jessica?'

She spread her hands, refusing to take the question seriously. 'I've found my family, I have a good job— what more could I want?'

'A man of your own, maybe. From what I saw last night, Craig isn't exactly immune to his new-found cousin's charms. Not that I realised who the Arab was until later.' He grinned faintly. 'I have to confess to feeling a bit piqued when you took to the floor with him only minutes after turning me down.'

'Policy,' she disclaimed hurriedly. 'At that time I was still a simple employee.'

'Except that I saw your face when you were dancing. You didn't look like that over anyone else you danced with last night.'

'Can we talk about something else?' Jessica asked, low-toned, and wiped the smile right off Peter's face.

'Oh, lord, I'm sorry if I put my foot in it. I didn't realise . . .' He stopped, lifting his shoulders in a rueful little shrug. 'Looks as if we might both be in the same boat. Shall we go back inside?'

He apologised again when she was leaving around nine, having obviously spent the evening regretting his outspoken comments.

'I hope we can go on being friends,' he finished.

'Of course,' Jessica assured him, wishing she had had the sense to laugh off the whole situation while she had the chance. 'I enjoyed today, Peter. Thanks for inviting me.'

'Mum said you were to come any time you had a mind,' he reminded her. 'She means it. So do I.' He shut the car door for her and stepped back, lifting a hand in fleeting salute, as she pulled away down the drive.

Jessica had spoken the truth in saying she had enjoyed the past few hours, yet she was glad now to be on her own again. The night was clear, the air balmy. She wound down her window the better to savour it. If she headed south she could be in London within a few hours, she mused. Janet would let her sleep at the flat, even if it did mean using the sofa. She knew she was being ridiculous. Almost all she possessed in the world was back at Morley. And what about Louise? She had promised to stay, and stay she would, Craig or no Craig. How long for she had no idea. As long as she could stand it, she imagined.

The Plough appeared to be doing good business when she passed through the village, the car park almost filled to capacity. Off the beaten track though the place was, the local brew attracted many outsiders at the weekends. A regular little goldmine, according to Leo, who prided himself on being a connoisseur of all public houses in the area. A small group of the village men chatted on the pavement outside the open doors, and they all turned to watch the car pass before going back to their conversation.

It was halfway up the hill that the engine died on her. Jessica stepped hastily on the brake and allowed the vehicle to run backwards down a few feet into the hedge bottom before applying the handbrake with a sense of *déjà vu*. This time, however, the cause of the breakdown took little working out. The petrol gauge showed as near empty as it could get. Of all the stupid things to happen this had to be the worst, she acknowledged ruefully. She had meant to fill up on the way over to Peter's, but had passed no station to give her the reminder.

The one in the village had been closed just now, which left her with very little choice. The house lay perhaps a couple of miles from here, with another half-mile trek up the drive, but there was nothing else for it unless she wanted to sit here all night.

The heels of her shoes were not made for walking very far. After the crossroads she took them off and walked on the grass verge in her stockinged feet, trusting to luck not to step in or on anything nasty. The sound of a car coming up fast behind her gave her pause for a moment, though in her white dress she could hardly fail to be seen. A lift would be very welcome, she reflected, turning to watch the approaching headlights—always providing she wouldn't be jumping into more trouble by accepting one, that was. A dark country lane was hardly the place to be hitching rides.

Half blinded by the powerful headlights, she failed to recognise the car until it was almost on top of her. Craig pulled to a stop beside her and leaned across to open the passenger door, face austere in the interior lighting.

'Get in,' he ordered.

Jessica did so because there was little other choice, pulling on her sandals before closing the door again. 'I ran out of petrol,' she said, donning a deliberately flippant tone. 'Stupid of me, wasn't it?'

'Very.' He put the Mercedes into motion without looking at her, accelerating smoothly. 'I saw the car back there on the hill. You were lucky you got as close to home as you did.'

'Or unlucky that I didn't make it another couple of miles,' she came back still on the same note. 'Actually, it's a lovely night for a walk. I was quite enjoying it.'

'I'm sure you were.' He sounded sardonic. 'Let's dispense with the small talk, shall we?'

'Anything you say,' Jessica put her head back against the rest and closed her eyes, determined to stay on top of the situation. 'Wake me when we get there.'

He was silent after that, but she could feel his presence. Inevitably she found herself recalling the previous night, trembling at the memory of his lovemaking and subsequent attack. Unfinished business, Craig had called it this morning, but he had been good and angry at the time. No doubt he would have had second thoughts by now.

They seemed to be a long time reaching the gates. Jessica opened her eyes and lifted her head to look through the windscreen, seeing nothing but darkness beyond the beam of the headlights. She sat up straighter with a jerk, turning to glance out through the rear screen to the lights of the house visible through the trees.

'Where are you going?' she demanded on a rising inflection. 'The house is back there!'

'I'm well aware of it.' Craig didn't bother to look in her direction, the line of his jaw indicative of his mood. 'We'll go back when I say so.'

After I'm through with you: he didn't need to say it, the implication was clear as day. Jessica felt her pulses quicken, her muscles tense. He hadn't forgotten—or forgiven.

'Where's the point in carrying things any further?' she asked, trying to stay cool and collected in a situation fast moving beyond her control. 'There must be plenty of women both ready and willing to give you what you think you missed out on last night.'

'Could be,' he agreed. 'Only they wouldn't provide the same satisfaction. The sooner we reach an understanding the better as far as I'm concerned.'

'Punishment for daring to deceive the head of the house?' Her tone was derisive. 'We already have an understanding. How about mutual contempt?'

He made no immediate answer, slowing the car to turn off the road into a narrow lane overhung with trees and bring it to a stop, switching off the lights as he did so.

'We'll be uninterrupted here,' he said.

Jessica looked at him for a long, disturbing moment in the darkness, seeing the set of his mouth with a tremor of awareness. There was no fear in her, only a rising excitation; an arousal she couldn't control. She wanted him to make love to her, she realised; she wanted it to the exclusion of everything else. From somewhere she found the willpower to make one faint protest. 'You'll regret this, Craig. We'll both regret it!'

'Maybe. We shan't know until it's too late.'

He reached for her then, fingers steely at her back. There was no gentleness in his kiss, nor did she want it. She responded blindly, crushed by the hardness of his chest and relishing the pain. Somewhere at the back of her mind lay the knowledge that she was being a fool in allowing this to happen, but she refused to let it matter. Desire overrode caution all the way down the line.

Craig did something to the seat backs, dropping them into line with the rear squab and laying her flat.

'Don't fight me,' he said softly as she made an involuntary move to escape his descending weight. 'This time I'm not taking no for an answer.'

She had no real intention of saying it, too far gone to repulse the emotions running through her body. It had merely been a token gesture on her part—an unspoken need to have any decision taken from her. She ran her hands up inside the silk of his shirt, curling her fingers into the mat of hair before sliding them over muscular shoulders to hold him close in total abandonment.

The buttons of her dress came undone easily. She was wearing little beneath, her skin gleaming palely against the darker tan of his hands. Craig put his lips to her breasts, springing each nipple erect with darting flicks of his tongue and bringing a tiny moan of pure agony from deep within her. Her legs moved of their own accord to accommodate him, her body lifting to take him into her with a sense of completion, as if some essential part of her hitherto missing had finally found its home. The minutes ran together, dissolving into one timeless interval when the whole world tilted on its axis and spun them both endlessly into space.

Reaction hit her only when Craig finally eased himself away from her prior to sitting up. A shaft of moonlight caught his profile, highlighting the chiselled line of mouth and chin. He looked untouched by any depth of emotion.

'We need to talk,' he said. 'Do you want to do it here or back at the house?'

'What is there to say?' Her voice sounded dead, all expression washed from it. 'You got what you were after.'

'Not wholly.' He still didn't look at her, resting an elbow on the wheel to gaze out through the windscreen at black foliage. 'I've a proposition to put to you.'

'I thought you already had.' She came up on one elbow, pulling the white dress about her as she did so. The pleasure had flown along with every atom of self-respect. Right now she wanted nothing more than to escape from this car—from this whole unsavoury mess. She said huskily, 'It's finished, Craig. I'm not going to become a commodity for your use whenever you happen to feel like it!'

'Not even if a wedding ring goes with it?'

It took a minute or two for the words to sink in. Jessica could only stare at him, unable to believe she had heard correctly.

'Is that meant to be a joke?' she got out at last.

His lips twisted. 'If it was the joke could very well finish up on me. No, I'm serious enough.'

'Why?' The word was a whisper. '*Why*, Craig?'

'Because if I'm going to take a wife at all I'd as soon it was one I can enjoy having,' he came back with irony. 'You're far from the cool customer you try to make out, Jessica. In fact, I'd go so far as to say you're one of the most responsive females I've ever known.'

'The voice of experience,' she sneered, but her heart wasn't in the jibe. 'That still doesn't explain why you're asking me to marry you.'

'Expediency,' he said. 'I want a son to inherit Morley from me. We're third cousin's, there's no genetic reason why we shouldn't . . .'

'The word is breed,' she cut in brusquely. 'One way

of keeping the strain pure, I suppose!' She drew in a painful breath, feeling the ache deep down. 'Thanks, but no, thanks. If and when I marry it will be to a man I can respect!'

'You'd get as much out of it as I would.' He seemed unmoved by anything she had said. 'Tonight was hardly the ultimate experience, considering the circumstances. Imagine what we could achieve given the choice of time and place.'

Jessica could, only too clearly. Craig would never be a man to make love in any cursory fashion, regardless of circumstances. He was too much of the sensualist. Her own senses stirred afresh to the memory of his hands and lips on her body, the shattering culmination. She wanted him again right now, this very moment. It was all she could do to stop herself from showing that desire in her eyes, in her voice, in the very unsteadiness of her limbs.

'I said no and I mean no,' she forced out through clenched teeth. 'Now can we go home?'

'If I have to keep you here all night I'll do it,' he responded hardily. 'Think what you'd gain. As my wife you'd be mistress of Morley, with all that entails.'

'Under your jurisdiction.'

'Let's call it guidance. And that would only apply to certain aspects. In all other respects you'd be entirely your own mistress.' He used the word with satire. 'All I want is a mother for my son.'

'There have to be others better equipped than I am to fill that role,' Jessica protested on a note of desperation. 'What about Caroline?'

'Caroline has other interests.'

'You mean she isn't prepared to accept the conditions.'

'I don't know,' he said. 'I've never asked her.'

It was a moment before she found a reply to that one. 'Blood not rich enough? Mine's diluted, remember.

Supposing my father's genes came through?'

'A risk I'm prepared to take.'

'Well, I'm not!'

'You'd rather leave Morley altogether.'

She said flatly, 'You promised your mother I could stay. Would you like to see her hurt?'

'No,' he admitted. There was a faint change of expression in his eyes, a flicker come and gone. 'Would you?'

'No, I wouldn't. Which is why I shan't be telling her what kind of son she really has.' She moved to the edge of her seat, finding the lever which controlled the lowering mechanism and springing the backrest into position. 'Just take me back.'

'If you insist.' The capitulation came with a shrug. 'We'll discuss it some other time.'

'The answer will be the same.'

'We'll see.' Craig put his own seat back up and started the engine, reversing out from the shelter of the trees to turn the car round and head back up the hill.

It was gone half past eleven when they reached the house. Craig slid the car in neatly at the side of the Ferrari and followed Jessica indoors. Beth came out from the library to the sound of the closing door, a book in her hand. There was a tremulous quality to her smile of greeting.

'Hi,' she said. 'Did you enjoy your tea with the Turners, Jessica?'

'Very much,' Jessica responded. Something in the younger girl's eyes prompted an unrehearsed addition. 'Peter sends his love.'

Colour came and went in Beth's face, her glance fleetingly meeting that of her brother as he moved past her to the door behind her. 'That was—nice of him.'

Craig spoke without turning his head. 'I'm going to have a nightcap. Anyone feel like joining me?'

'I was just going up,' disclaimed his sister.

He paused in the doorway, looking back to where Jessica stood at the foot of the stairs, cynicism written in the curve of his lips. 'How about you?'

She gazed at him dully, hating herself more than him because she actually wanted to be with him. 'No,' she said without bothering to conceal her feelings. 'Goodnight, Beth.'

The girl caught her up on the gallery, falling into step beside her. 'Did you and Craig have a row?' she asked curiously. 'You sounded so short with him just now.'

'He resents my coming here without announcing who I really was,' Jessica acknowledged with truth. 'I suppose I did go about things in a rather ridiculous fashion.'

'I don't think so. You'd a right to want to know what you might be letting yourself in for.' Beth stopped at her own bedroom door, smile tentative. 'I'm glad you came, Jessica.'

'Really?' Jessica's voice was gentle. 'That's nice of you.' Her pause held deliberation. 'You know, Peter and I really are just friends. All he talks about is you.'

'Does he?' Animation lit the grey eyes for a moment, then as swiftly faded again. 'It's no use. Craig is quite right. I'm just not ready to get married. Not to anyone.'

'Why not explain that to Peter and ask him to just let things ride for the present?' suggested Jessica. 'I'm sure he'd understand.'

'You really think so?' There was doubt in the question. 'I'm not even all that sure I understand myself.' Beth paused, looking at her cousin with something like entreaty. 'You see, I still feel the same way about him. When he was dancing with you last night I wanted to come and take him away, only I'd already told him I didn't want to see him again. He's very good at his job, you know—even Craig agrees with that. He could have specialised, only he preferred general practice.' She stopped again, her expression suddenly wry. 'I don't really fit the image, do I?'

'Not at the moment,' Jessica was bound to agree. 'But that isn't to say you couldn't in the future. It needs thinking about, that's all.'

'Yes.' Beth sounded rueful. 'I certainly didn't do much of that before. To be honest, I don't think I saw much farther than actually getting married. Do you know what I mean?'

'Yes.' The acknowledgement was forced. Marriage was the last thing Jessica felt like discussing right now. 'Anyway, have a sleep on it.'

That piece of advice was one she was to wish she could follow herself during the hours following while she lay tossing and turning in bed. Thinking back over everything Craig had said to her, she had to admit to temptation regardless of all his proposal lacked. Her own mistress during the day and his at night, that was what it amounted to. In actual fact, she stood to gain more from the arrangement than he did. Plenty of quite successful marriages had been contracted without love; in some Eastern countries that emotion was accorded the least consideration. There was even the possibility that love might develop between them over a period.

Honesty compelled her to acknowledge that unlikely. Craig didn't appear capable of any depth of emotion where women were concerned. They were there to be used, in any capacity he should happen to choose. Her function would be to please him in bed and bear his children.

Inevitably she found herself imagining what it might be like to have Craig's child. It would have to be a boy; with Craig for a father it wouldn't dare turn out to be anything else. A redhead like her—or darker like his father? Would he have green eyes or grey? Mark was a good name for a boy. Mark Stafford. He would grow up tall, of course. All the Stafford men were tall.

She had to stop this, she told herself almost feverishly at that point. Any relationship between a man and a woman needed to be founded on something solid in order to have any chance at all; if not love then at least some depth of liking and respect. Tonight Craig had taken her as ruthlessly as he would go after any contract in which he saw a profit to be made. If she had refused him he would very likely have used force. But then he had known she wouldn't be refusing him—or certainly not for long. He had been fully aware from the first moment of their meeting just how he affected her. Last night he had wanted her simply because she was there and seemingly available. Certainly there would have been no offer of marriage to follow the seduction he had planned. As Emma's granddaughter she had suddenly become a different proposition—her breeding no longer open to doubt.

I hate him, she thought, and knew it wasn't true. How could she hate a man who could make her feel the way Craig made her feel? Even now she ached for him; longed for his touch, for his lips claiming hers; for the lean, hard weight of his body. If the first time had been so utterly wonderful what would it be like the second, and the third—to lie in his arms every night? Loving and making love were not necessarily synonymous; for the average male physical expression was more than enough. Were women really so different when it came right down to it? Couldn't she bring herself to admit she could manage without love?

She slept eventually, wakening to sunlight and a renewal of doubt. She couldn't marry Craig—not if she wanted to retain what self-respect he had left her. If he started the same nonsense again she would be ready for him.

CHAPTER EIGHT

JESSICA skipped breakfast, reluctant to face Craig until she absolutely had to. Bob Grainger was already in the office when she got there. He greeted her in surprise.

'You're an early bird this morning!'

'I didn't feel like eating,' Jessica explained lamely, 'so I came right over. I never saw you at the Ball on Saturday.'

'Margaret didn't feel up to it,' he said, 'and I didn't feel like coming without her.

'I hope she isn't ill.'

'A nervous complaint,' he admitted. 'Had it for years. Did you enjoy yourself?'

'Oh yes.' She could hardly say anything else. Her hesitation was brief; Bob had to know some time. 'I have a confession to make,' she added. 'I'm Emma Stafford's granddaughter.'

'That was the one who ran off to get married, wasn't it?' He sounded interested but not particularly surprised. 'I always thought it odd that you and young Beth should have the same colouring. It isn't all that common a shade of hair. Family accept it all right, did they?'

'It appears so.' She wondered what he might say if he only knew the truth of the matter. She smiled brightly. 'At any rate, I'm being allowed to keep my job for the present.'

'That's a relief. We might find it difficult, getting someone else to take over from you.' He paused, eyes on the paper he held in his hand. 'Did Craig stay over?'

'Yes.' Carefully she added, 'There was some talk of him spending a week or so.'

'That's good. There are one or two things I want to discuss with him.' He glanced up as the outer door opened. 'Well, I'll be blessed! We were just talking about you!'

'Telepathy?' Craig suggested with the merest hint of irony. 'I thought my ears were burning.' He glanced over to where Jessica stood in the inner office doorway, expression unrevealing. 'Mother is anxious to see you. I said I'd send you back across if you turned out to be here. On a diet, are we?'

She refused to acknowledge the latter remark, eyeing him back with all the equanimity she could muster. 'Did she say it had to be now?'

'I gathered that was what she'd prefer.' He held open the door for her. 'I'm sure Bob won't mind sparing you for half an hour.'

Under the circumstances there was little else she could do but comply, doubtful as she was of the urgency of the request. Craig was simply underlining the fact that if she stayed on at all it would be purely for his mother's sake. Her turning down of the offer he had made her last night must have been a real blow to his pride, even if he didn't appear to be smarting under it on the surface.

He stayed to talk with Bob while Jessica returned to the house, meeting up with Leo in the rear passage.

'Mother's in the morning room,' he said in answer to her query. 'She's all excited over something, though she won't say what exactly. What made you miss breakfast?'

'Lack of appetite,' she said over her shoulder. 'I'll make up for it at lunch.'

Louise was standing at the long window looking out over the grounds when Jessica ran her to earth. She turned at her entry, eyes lighting up with a warmth and delight she could obviously barely contain.

'Oh, my dear, I can't tell you how pleased I am! I

could scarcely believe it when Craig came and told me this morning before breakfast. The two of you must have done a lot of thinking since Saturday night. I'm so glad you both realised that the relationship was too far removed to make any difference to your feelings for each other.' She held out her hands. 'Come over here and let me kiss my future daughter-in-law.'

Dazedly Jessica forced her feet to obey the injunction, aware that Craig had found the one sure way of forcing her hand. After a reaction like this, how could she possibly turn round and tell Louise she had been misled? He had put her in a cleft stick, her only alternative to go along with the story. She tried to smile, to look like a bride-to-be might be expected to look, while mentally condemning the man responsible for this whole affair. He had got his own way after all, regardless of what she wanted.

'I hoped this would happen,' Louise admitted, drawing her to a seat in the window bottom. 'From almost the first day you came to Morley I knew you were a special kind of girl. It's good to realise that Craig thinks so too. Not that I ever anticipated such a swift decision on his part. He tells me you neither of you want to wait too long, but I had to point out to him that a wedding can't be arranged in five minutes either. You'll be married at Holy Trinity in Skipton, of course—the Staffords always are. Can you let me have a list of guests you'll be wanting to invite as soon as possible? I know it sounds as if I'm rushing things, but engraving takes so much time.' She paused for breath, laughing at Jessica's bemused expression. 'You'll have to forgive me for running on like this. I've so wanted Craig to find himself a wife who'd make him happy, and I'm sure he has. I've seen that special look in your eyes when you've spoken about him—particularly this last week while he's been away. Shall you mind his going away so much?'

'I haven't had time to think about it,' Jessica returned carefully. 'It's something we didn't get round to discussing yet.' She hesitated, hardly knowing how to carry this thing through. If there had been a time for retreat at all it was long past. 'Craig wants a son to carry on the line,' she said, in an attempt to impart some element of realism into the proceedings.

'Well, of course he does. A marriage isn't complete without children.' Louise's expression underwent a sudden change as a new thought struck her. She added diffidently, 'You *do* want children, don't you, Jessica?'

Jessica made the smile as natural as possible. 'Do you really think Craig would have asked me to marry him without making sure of that? Your son doesn't leave things to chance.'

'My son—your husband-to-be. I can still barely take it in! Craig suggested three weeks from Thursday for the wedding. It's going to be a rush, but we'll cope. Your dress will be the biggest headache. You're the first Stafford bride in thirty-six years, and the whole county is going to be agog. We have to give them a spectacle worthy of tradition.'

It was growing worse by the second. Jessica's teeth felt numb with the effort of clenching them together. Somehow she managed to get through the following fifteen minutes or so of planning, eventually making her escape on a plea of work still waiting to be done.

'Bob will definitely have to find another secretary now,' was Louise's parting comment.

Craig was just going into the study as she came out of the morning room. She followed him in, closing the door behind her with icy control to look across at him as he stood by the desk.

'Very neat,' she said. 'Tell me, has anyone ever got away with saying no to you?'

'Not often.' It was a bare statement of fact made without particular pride. The grey eyes were perfectly steady. 'Do I take it you're willing to play along?'

'No, I'm not willing. I don't want to marry you.' That wasn't wholly true, but this was no time to be splitting hairs. 'You deliberately put me in the position of having to choose between my peace of mind and your mother's. I'll never forgive you for that, Craig.'

'I'll survive.' He sounded totally unmoved. 'So will you. Be grateful you had the initiative taken out of your hands. This way you can always tell yourself you were forced into the whole situation.'

'So I was, right from the word go! You'd use anyone or anything to get what you want. Picking me up last night was a piece of sheer luck, wasn't it? The perfect opportunity handed to you on a platter. I wouldn't even put it past you to have syphoned off enough petrol to make sure I did run out before I got back here!'

'Except that I wouldn't have been able to count on your not noticing and filling up again on the way into Harrogate.' Craig's tone held derision. 'Don't let imagination run away with you. You were right the first time—it was sheer luck.'

'And you took full advantage.'

Dark brows lifted sardonically. 'I didn't notice you doing too much protesting at the time.'

There was warmth under her skin, but she ignored it. 'Shock tactics. I'm no more immune to them than the next. To be as good at your particular job as you obviously are, you have to be something of a psychologist—capable of weighing up a prospect on sight. All right, so you made me want you last night. Next time I might not be quite so accommodating.'

She had said the wrong thing there; the sudden dangerous glint in his eyes told her that much. He moved without haste but with certain purpose, pulling her away from the door to turn the key in the lock with a decisive click.

'Let's see about that, shall we?'

Jessica resisted with vigour as he propelled her across the room to the chesterfield by the fireplace, making little impression. Sitting down, he pulled her across his knees, holding her head still to find her mouth with unerring aim and inescapable compulsion. Jessica felt the immediate springing of response, and knew he felt it too. His hand slid inside her blouse, cupping her breast with a lightness of touch that made her tremble, arousing her so fast she could hardly get the words out.

'Not here, Craig. Please, not in here!'

'Then say it,' he said softly. 'Stop sticking your head in the sand and darn well *say* it!'

He had her trapped again, the choice entirely hers. Whichever way she made it he came out on top. Her voice was husky. 'So all right, I want you. Is that what you want to hear?'

'Again,' he ordered. 'I'm not sure I heard you. Try it again!'

She caught at his hand, staying its movement, her whole body tensed against the temptation to reverse her decision. 'I want you!' she said fiercely. '*Damn* you, Craig!'

His laugh had a cruel edge. 'We'll make something of this relationship of ours yet! Can I take it you won't be making any more hasty statements like that last one?'

'Yes.' Her brows were drawn together. 'You're hurting me!'

'You deserve a little pain.' He relaxed his hold on her, mouth taking on a slant. 'Maybe I should turn you over while I have the opportunity and teach you some elementary respect. We may not have a conventional arrangement, but we're going to have a certain understanding.'

Jessica curled her own lip in deliberate imitation. 'If that's the kind of thing you enjoy, go right ahead. I wouldn't give you the pleasure of trying to stop you!'

This time the smile was genuine. 'I'll say one thing for

you, you're not easily put down. I fancy I'd be wasting my time—to say nothing of energy. That's not to say I mightn't find some other method of bringing you to heel.'

'You said I'd be my own mistress,' she reminded him, forcing herself to lie still in his arms until he decided to let her go.

'I said in some respects. It's going to be up to you to strike the right balance. Regardless of how or why, I don't intend having a wife who treats me with any kind of contempt, especially in public. So far as the world is concerned, we'll be a normal, loving couple.'

'Don't sneer at love,' she retorted with alacrity, 'just because you don't understand that kind of emotion.'

'And you do?' Craig studied her for a moment, his expression hard to decipher. 'Were you in love with this man you left your last job because of?'

'I thought I was.' Her voice was taut.

'But you've realised since that the grand passion wasn't so grand after all.' He shook his head, mouth mocking again. 'It doesn't last, Jessica. Believe me, I've tried it. It dulls the intellect for a start—makes it difficult to form any true judgment of character. A few years ago I really thought I'd found my soulmate. She had me going round in circles for weeks until I woke up and realised she was just another pretty face.'

'That wasn't love,' she said, 'it was infatuation.'

'Tell me the difference.'

'I wouldn't even attempt it.' Jessica stirred restlessly. 'Can I get up now?'

'Why not?' Craig got up himself, putting her back on her feet. 'There you are—unsullied and safe. We're taking a trip into town after lunch. We have to see about a ring. Do you have any preference in stones?'

'Diamonds,' she said with deliberation. 'The bigger the better. How about a nice flashy three-carat solitaire? I could have my nose pierced just to be different!'

Surprisingly his lips twitched. 'That reckless streak is going to get you into trouble one of these fine days. You'll take what you get. Just be ready to leave at two. Incidentally, I had your car fetched in by the local garage. We'll see about finding you something more suitable.'

'You mean befitting my position?' she retorted shortly. 'I don't suppose it occurred to you that I might prefer to keep the Mini.'

'It was five years old and starting to rust,' he pointed out with unexpected tolerance. 'You can use one of the estate cars until we get you fixed up.'

It was useless protesting. Her life was no longer her own. She tried not to listen to the small voice that whispered that it could even be worth the sacrifice.

The rest of the family were told the news at lunchtime, eliciting reactions varying from the startled to the frankly disbelieving. Beth was obviously more than a little confused, considering what she had noted the previous night. Jessica gave her a smiling little shrug as if in apology for any false impressions given, disliking the deception but not about to put Beth in the position of having to pretend with her mother. So far as the younger girl would be concerned she and Craig had made up their differences after she herself had gone to bed.

Great-Uncle Philip was the first to show approval, taking his cue from his niece's pleasure. It took Leo to make the most honest comment, his face reflecting a wry acceptance. 'Life is full of surprises. I suppose this means we'll need another secretary in the estate office?'

'I can fill in until you find someone,' Jessica offered quickly.

'Only on a part-time basis, I'm afraid,' put in Louise. 'You're going to be taken up with all kinds of things this next couple of weeks. Tomorrow, you have to be measured for your dress. The only people I'd trust with the making are in York. They're sending out a fitter. She'll bring some designs with her to give you an idea of what you might like. Unfortunately the choice is going to be limited by the time available.'

'She could get married in sackcloth and set a new trend,' suggested Leo blandly, and drew a quelling glance from his brother.

'Let's cut out the smart remarks, shall we? You're going to be trying on yourself before the week's out.'

'You're not considering having me for best man, I hope?'

'No,' came the unmoved response. 'I'll be bringing Jake Loxley down for that job.'

Jessica smiled across at Beth, feeling it was time she took a hand in arrangements, no matter what the doubts still in her mind. 'Will you be my chief bridesmaid?' She forced a laugh. 'My only bridesmaid, actually—I don't have anyone else to ask.'

'What about your friends in London?' Louise queried. 'Surely there's someone you'd like to have?'

'Not that I feel close enough to.' Jessica was determined not to be moved on that point. 'I'd hate to be followed down the aisle by a whole retinue, anyway.' She caught Craig's eye, surprising a faint but unmistakable sympathy. She had to concentrate to remember what she had been going to say. 'You realise I don't have anyone to give me away? I suppose someone has to.'

'Uncle Philip can do it,' Louise announced comfortably. 'He's your great-uncle too, so it won't be unfitting.'

The senior member of the Stafford household looked gratified, his interest in the whole affair suddenly taking on new life. 'Emma would have been pleased,' he said with some complacency. 'She and I were always very close.'

It was her grandmother Jessica found herself thinking about while driving into town later. Would she have approved of what was happening, she wondered, or would she have condemned any marriage contracted under such conditions? She had loved her own husband with a depth of feeling that had cancelled out all other considerations. Family, friends, and security had all been sacrificed. More than just a physical relationship, for certain, although that too must have played its part. Grandfather had been such a gentle man—not in any way like Craig. Yet could a gentle man satisfy her the way Craig could satisfy her? Perhaps she needed strength both of mind and matter in order to find a true fulfilment. Humour touched her for a fleeting moment. It was certainly what she was getting anyway.

Craig glanced her way curiously. 'What are you smiling at?'

'Nothing you'd appreciate,' she said. 'Perhaps I was just reconciling myself to the inevitable.'

'Perhaps as well, considering I don't intend letting you get away from me,' he came back dryly. 'By the way, you'll need to take a look at the room we'll be sharing. It hasn't been used since my father died—Mother said it held too many memories.'

'Good ones, I imagine?'

'It's a debatable point. My father wasn't an easy man to live with. He mellowed a little when he knew he was dying, but Mother never had much of a life of her own.'

'You mean theirs was a marriage of expediency too,' Jessica said softly. 'At least on your father's part. What happens if I only give you daughters?'

'The Stafford men have always fathered more sons than daughters,' he returned imperturbably. 'Your grandmother was the first girl in three generations, Beth is only the second in four. I'd say the odds were on my side.'

'They'd have to be,' she agreed. 'You don't play long shots, do you, Craig?'

'Not if I can avoid it.' He glanced at her again, his expression unreadable. 'I can't afford the luxury.'

The jeweller's to which he took her was small and exclusive, the items on display in the Georgian windows bearing no price tags. The manager was expecting them, taking them through to the rear office to produce several trays of rings for their approval.

It was Craig who picked up the huge diamond solitaire for Jessica to try, his mouth tilting as he did so. 'Not quite three carats,' he said, 'but close enough. Does it take your fancy?'

On her hand the ring looked flashy and ostentatious. With some deliberation she picked out a small single stone surrounded by tiny sapphires, slipping it on to her finger and holding it out to admire. 'How about this one?'

'From the sublime to the ridiculous.' There was an element of impatience in the comment. 'I like the cluster you just hesitated over. The setting is perfect.'

Jessica thought so too, yet still prevaricated. In the end it was Craig himself who took the ring from the tray and slipped it on to her finger, keeping a hold on her hand.

'We'll take that one,' he said. 'And we'd better look at wedding rings too while we're here.'

'Are you planning on wearing one?' Jessica asked in surprise as the manager went to fetch a selection, and received a dry smile.

'Why not? The contract is effective both ways.'

Her shrug was light. 'I suppose it will save you the trouble of tying a knot in your handkerchief.'

The matching wedding rings had to be left to be engraved, but the other they took with them. Once in the car, Craig insisted that she put it on, watching her with cynicism as she did so.

'Now it's official,' he said. 'We'll have champagne at

dinner tonight—unless you feel you'd like to go out somewhere to celebrate.'

'Celebrate what?' asked Jessica with intent. 'Your mother is the only reason I'm going through with this at all.'

The grey eyes held mockery. 'The *only* reason?'

'That's right.' She returned his gaze without flinching. 'You're not the only man capable of performing a biological function, Craig—or of making me enjoy it!'

'I'd better be.' The mockery had gone, replaced by something infinitely more meaningful. 'Don't ever make the mistake of experimenting with comparisons, Jessica. You wouldn't like what would happen to you one little bit.'

She could believe it. The Stafford pride was not to be lightly pricked. 'Don't worry,' she said. 'I've agreed to marry you and I'll stick to the rules. Just so long as we understand one another, that's all.'

He reached out then to start the engine up, expression controlled. 'I'd say we do that very well.'

That was the evening Louise insisted on giving up her place at one end of the dining table in deference to Jessica.

'You may as well start getting used to it,' she said, firmly brushing aside Jessica's protests. 'As mistress of the house that's where you're going to belong.'

'Tradition,' put in Leo on a drawling note. 'You can't escape it, Jess. Not in this house.'

'Her name,' said his brother coolly from the head of the table, 'is Jessica. Try it.'

'You don't mind, do you?' appealed the younger man, looking at his future sister-in-law with lifted brows. 'It comes more naturally, that's all.'

She hesitated, torn between honesty and reluctance to let him down. 'I don't think it's important,' she said at last, avoiding Craig's eyes. Her smile was light. 'Call me what you like, providing it isn't rude!'

'The Agency is sending a couple for interview on Wednesday,' said Louise into the brief silence following. 'I think you should be the one to see them, Jessica.'

'I wouldn't know what to look for,' she protested in some dismay. 'You can't just throw me in at the deep end, like that! What kind of questions am I supposed to ask?'

The other woman laughed and shook her head. 'All right, I'll do it. You'd better be there too, though. The way Pauline has been acting this last week or two I'd say you're going to be interviewing to replace her before very long—always providing we manage to find any applicants at all.'

'Well, Morley isn't exactly handy for off-duty entertainments, is it?' said Beth reasonably. 'Pauline likes to go to the disco, only the nearest one is in Skipton and the bus service out this direction finishes at ten. Even then she's left with about a mile to walk on her own, and you know what can happen to girls in country lanes at night.'

Jessica wanted suddenly to laugh. Did she ever! Craig was watching her without expression.

'We seem to be left with two alternatives,' he stated. 'Either find someone older, or provide Pauline with transport to and from her source of entertainment.'

'A pity you got rid of my Mini,' suggested Jessica blandly. 'She could have had the use.'

'I doubt if she can drive.' He obviously had no intention of rising to the taunt. 'Anyway, you can sort out that particular problem.'

'Among others.' Leo sounded just faintly malicious. 'I hope you have plenty of stamina.'

She was going to need all of that, she acknowledged in wry acceptance.

It was after dinner, when Craig was temporarily

absent, that Leo took the opportunity to corner her on her own, perching on the arm of her chair in a way that cut them off from the rest of the room.

'I'm not sure what's been going on,' he said, 'but one thing I am sure of. You're not going to find any of it a bed of roses.' Blue eyes oddly hurt, he added plaintively, 'You might at least have dropped a hint about you and Craig. I thought we were friends.'

'We are,' she said. 'I hope we're going to go on being friends.'

He didn't seem to have heard. 'He's using you, you know. He uses everybody, one way or another. If he doesn't get himself a son and heir I stand to inherit the place from him when he dies, and there's no way he's going to let that happen.'

Jessica met his gaze squarely. 'You can hardly blame him for that, can you? After all, you've never shown much interest in keeping the estate up to scratch.'

The wince was genuine, his expression suddenly wry. 'You don't exactly temper judgment with mercy, do you?'

'Do you think you deserve it?' she asked. 'Come on, Leo, be honest. You've absolutely no feeling for Morley or all it stands for. You'd be better on your own somewhere.'

'Except that I can't do it without help.' His manner had changed, a certain hope dawning. 'You obviously have influence with Craig. Can't you persuade him to find me some opening?'

'I'll try.' It was all she could say; he wouldn't believe her if she told him the truth. Influence with Craig? That was a hope! She doubted if he would even bother to listen.

He had returned to the room while the two of them had been talking. Catching sight of his face as he sat down opposite, she knew their tête-à-tête was not appreciated. So let him stew, she thought judiciously.

One thing he was not going to do was rule her life completely.

Louise was the first to break up the evening with the announcement that she felt ready for bed. Beth retired soon afterwards, and Leo wandered off somewhere, leaving Jessica and Craig alone with Uncle Philip, who showed no sign of moving from his favourite chair.

'Perhaps it's time we went up too,' said Craig after several minutes. 'It's been a heavy day.' He got to his feet, sliding his hands into his trouser pockets as he stood looking down at her where she sat. 'Coming?'

'Leaving me on my own, are you?' grumbled Philip Stafford comfortably. 'Well, it will be nice to have some peace and quiet for a few minutes before I go to bed myself.'

Crossing the hall, Craig said with decision, 'We'd better contact the Agency in Harrogate and get someone out here on a temporary basis until your job can be filled. You're not going to have time to give it your full attention.'

'What if they don't have anyone available?' asked Jessica.

'Then Leo will have to start pulling his weight for once, like it or not.' His glance was calculated. 'Don't bother saying it. If Leo wants out he has the option any time. His income would be more than adequate, providing he sold the Ferrari and settled for a reasonable standard of living.'

'Supposing the positions had been reversed?' Jessica suggested, trying to keep the conversation on an unemotive level. 'Is that what you would have done?'

'I certainly shouldn't have stayed to watch Morley fall apart through lack of care and attention.' He shook his head impatiently. 'What difference does it make? It didn't happen that way. Leo isn't your concern, Jessica, I'd like you to remember that.'

There was no answer she could make—none, at least,

that bore any weight. Leo, unfortunately, would have to carry his own banner.

Reaching the gallery a step ahead of Craig, she was reminded of that other night not so long ago when he had followed her up the stairs. Had anyone told her then that in two short weeks she would be engaged to marry the same man she would have laughed at them. What was she doing here anyway?

She knew the moment he touched her, turning her around to face him with his hands lightly at her waist. There was an odd look in the grey eyes.

'Considering the way things are, I don't think it's going to do either of us any harm to wait three weeks before we start spending nights together,' he said, 'so we'll part right here. Any objections?'

She shook her head numbly, knowing it wasn't true. Only when she was with him could she forget what was lacking in their relationship to any great extent. Three weeks of lonely nights meant three weeks of thinking and regretting. She only hoped she could take it. But she had to take it, didn't she? The alternative left her with nothing.

CHAPTER NINE

LOOKING back afterwards, it was surprising how fast those three weeks passed. There was so much to do, so many arrangements to be made, so many people to meet. Gradually Jessica acquired a second skin against the occasional barbed remark, the speculation. Her reasons for marrying Craig were her own and nothing to do with anyone else. If slowly but surely her emotions were becoming more deeply involved then that too was her own affair. Loving Craig made things easier not harder, even if he didn't return the feeling.

There was no telling what Craig's thoughts might be; his moods were unpredictable. There was little intimacy of any kind between them even when the opportunity was there. Yet on the one occasion when she took the plunge and asked him bluntly if he wanted to call the whole thing off he was emphatic in his denial. They were going to be married, he said, come what may.

Louise seemed to have gained a whole new lease of life, dealing with caterers and florists, with dressmakers and milliners as if she were enjoying every moment. She bullied Jessica into buying a complete new wardrobe of clothes for her trousseau, pointing out that Craig would be providing her with security from now on, in which case the few hundred pounds she had saved was hardly going to be needed. Faced with displays of beautiful filmy lingerie, Jessica took little persuading. Whatever Craig's feelings—or lack of them—for her he could hardly fail to be stirred to some measure by the sheer invitation of floating black lace, the smooth sheen of silk.

They were motoring up to Scotland after the

wedding, much to the disgust of Louise who thought they should have chosen somewhere more exotic for a honeymoon. Craig didn't want to be away more than a week, explained Jessica on more than one occasion, but it made little difference. To her future mother-in-law this was a once-only affair and should be treated as such. Jessica only hoped she was not going to be disappointed in that belief. Time alone would tell.

Beth had been very quiet about the whole affair, although entering into the preparations when required. It took a moment some three days before the wedding when she and Jessica were alone together on the terrace to finally bring her to the point of talking about it.

'What I can't understand,' she said with some diffidence, 'is how you and Craig could be like enemies one day and engaged to be married the next. That night you came home together you looked as if you hated him.'

'I did,' Jessica confessed, deciding that a half truth was better than none. 'Right at that moment, anyway. I was angry with him—and he with me.'

'But you obviously made it up later!'

'We made it up next morning.'

'It must have been early. Mummy said Craig came to tell her the news before breakfast that morning.' Beth stole a swift glance. 'Oh, it's all right, I'm not shocked or anything. I read somewhere that the best place to settle a lovers' tiff was in bed.'

'Did you?' Jessica scarcely knew what else to say. She had the feeling that any denials on her part were not going to be believed. 'Have you seen anything of Peter?' she asked.

'Yes.' Animation sprang in both eyes and voice. 'We had a long talk.'

'And?'

'He's prepared to wait as long as I want him to.'

'That's nice.' Jessica waited a moment or two before

adding tentatively, 'Are you going to tell Craig you're seeing him again?'

The animation faded a little. 'If I don't Peter says he will. I suppose he's right. We can hardly keep it a secret. I'm of age, after all.'

'I'm sure Craig recognises that much,' said Jessica, wondering if she was right. 'He has nothing against Peter personally, it's just that he doesn't . . .'

'Doesn't see me as a doctor's wife,' Beth finished for her. 'To be honest, neither do I at present, but things can change. Or perhaps we'll both meet someone more suitable in the end. Who knows?'

Who indeed? acknowledged Jessica wryly. Her own future was scarcely more secure, unless she produced the son Craig wanted.

Her wedding day could not have been lovelier, with the sun shining from a cloudless blue sky and the temperature already climbing into the low seventies by eleven o'clock. With the ceremony at two-thirty, there was time for a light luncheon snack before going up to prepare. Jessica ate little, her nerves stretched to breaking point. Ridiculous to get this worked up over an arrangement as lacking in romance as theirs, yet she couldn't help herself. In a few hours' time she would be Mrs Craig Stafford, with all that entailed. She could still hardly believe it was really happening.

Craig had stayed the night in Skipton along with his best man. She wondered how he was feeling right now. Last night he had given her the string of finely matched pearls which was his wedding present, fastening them about her neck with a light touch and an even lighter comment. 'Pearls for tears,' he had said, 'but not for us. We both know exactly what we're doing, don't we, Jessica? And why.'

I'm doing this because I love you, she had wanted to say, but the words wouldn't come. They were not, in any case, what he would have wanted to hear.

Her dress was classic in style and superb in detail right from the high round neckline down to the softly flowing skirt. Looking at herself in the mirror as Beth helped settle the clouds of veiling about her face, Jessica thought longingly of later when all this was over and she and Craig could be alone. Perhaps in his arms she could forget the missing elements and find comfort in his desire alone. Providing he still did desire her. These past weeks he had seemed so aloof, so restrained in his treatment of her. Could it be he had regretted his impulse yet hadn't known how to call things off? Who could be sure of what went on in that cool, controlled mind of his?

'You look beautiful,' said Beth softly. 'At a time like this I keep thinking "I wish it was me", but I know that's only the occasion getting to me. At least you don't have any problems that way, Jessica. You'll make an ideal wife for Craig.'

Louise said much the same thing when she came in to check that the two of them were ready, tears starting in her eyes as she kissed the girl who was soon to be her son's bride.

'Thank heaven you took it into your head to pay us that visit,' she said, 'or we might never have known you.' She briskened then. 'Beth and I have to leave now. Uncle Philip is waiting downstairs. You're to leave the house at two exactly to allow for traffic. That's in seven minutes' time. We'll see you at the church.'

And Craig would be waiting for her, resplendent with his top hat and tails. Nervous? Jessica doubted it. Hers were the fears and trepidations, hers and hers alone. Craig wouldn't be going through with this if he had changed his mind in any way.

Time moved in a series of impressions after that: arriving at church to the curious stares of the gathered crowd; walking down the aisle towards the tall, grey-clad back of a man so suddenly and completely a stranger; the journey back to Morley in the company of that same stranger; shaking hands in the reception line with the feeling that people must be going round and round again, there seemed so many. Caroline was there, smiling a smile of congratulation and introducing the thin-faced Frenchman whom Craig appeared already to know. 'My fiancé', she called him. It explained such a lot.

Eventually it was time to change for their Highland journey, although not all of it was to be accomplished in what was left of the day. That night they were to spend in a hotel somewhere near Penrith where they would dine before retiring. To what? Jessica wondered as the Mercedes pulled away down the drive to the waves and cheers of the assembled guests. She could barely remember what Craig's lovemaking felt like, it had been so long.

'Tired?' Craig asked as the silence stretched between them, not taking his eyes from the road ahead. 'Why don't you put the seat back down and take a nap? We'll be there in a couple of hours.'

Jessica did so, stirring memories of the last time she had lain like this. For all she knew the son he craved for might already be growing inside her, no more than a cell as yet but with all the characteristics of a Stafford. Made to order, she thought with cynicism. One only hoped the finished product conformed to specifications!

The hotel was built like a castle, standing on the banks of a small lake with evening-misted hills behind it. Inside was thick-carpeted luxury and restrained décor, the whole atmosphere redolent of wealth and good living.

Signing in as Mr and Mrs Stafford felt strange. Jessica wondered if the receptionist guessed they were honeymooners, but could see no sign of recognition in the man's demeanour. The suite to which they were shown was on the first floor overlooking the lake, consisting of a beautifully furnished bedroom and separate sitting room, with one of the largest bathrooms Jessica had ever seen.

'We're only staying the one night,' she protested when they were alone. 'Isn't all this rather a waste?'

'I like space,' said Craig dismissively. 'Did you want to go down to dinner or would you prefer it up here?'

Her hesitation was brief. To go downstairs meant facing people, and she wasn't ready to do that. Not just yet. Craig was being so calm and detached about the whole thing, as if he got himself married every day of his life. She hoped he wouldn't be bringing the same detachment to bed with him tonight.

'Up here,' she said, 'then we don't have to dress.'

'All right.' He nodded to the phone. 'Order what you fancy for say an hour's time. I'll have the same. I'm going to take a shower.'

He went through to the bedroom before she could answer, leaving her biting her lip. As bridegrooms went he left a whole lot to be desired. But if cool efficiency was what he wanted, cool efficiency was what he was going to get. She would make no further move towards putting their relationship on a more intimate footing.

It took bare minutes to order the light meal for two. The shower had stopped running when she went into the bedroom, but she could hear the sound of movement from beyond the other door. The room was lit only by the fast-dimming glow from the setting sun. Even as she went to the window the last rays vanished behind the far hills, leaving a spreading wave of colour across the skies. A breeze had sprung up, rippling the surface of the lake into molten gold. No setting could be more perfect, she told herself ruefully. It was only the situation that was wrong.

Behind her the bathroom door opened, but she didn't

turn her head, standing there with one hand on the curtain draw-cord, reluctant to shut out the view.

'Beautiful, isn't it?' she said.

'Very.' Craig was right behind her, hands sliding about her waist to turn her slowly towards him, eyes meeting hers with an expression that made her catch her breath. 'And so are you. I can't wait for the traditional moment. I want you now.'

The kiss was scorching, lighting her senses with a swiftness and vibrancy she couldn't resist. 'Dinner,' she murmured as he began to undress her. 'I ordered dinner!'

His laugh came low. 'The way I feel we'll be through long before it arrives! We have the whole night for the leisurely approach.'

Hunger leapt in her, sending her mouth seeking his with a passion equalling his own. She felt the response in him, the tensing of muscle and sinew as he slid an arm under her to lift her. He carried her across to the bed, stripping off the light silk robe he wore to come down beside her and gather her into his arms, moulding her to every hard angle of his body before crushing her beneath him with a demand that brooked no denial.

They stayed out the week in the end, both of them reluctant to leave a place which had everything anyone could want. Jessica drifted through the golden days like someone in a dream, living for the moment without concern for the future. Some time she was going to have to wake up, and she knew it, but while this lasted she didn't want to think, only to feel.

Craig was different too: more relaxed, even genial at times. They talked about everything under the sun, discovering interests they hadn't even suspected they shared, yet finding bones of contention into the bargain. Only once did they come close to any real disagreement, when Jessica made some casual remark regarding the way in which the temporary estate secretary seemed to have left Leo redundant again, drawing a caustic and unfair comment she could not allow to pass. After the resulting heated exchange she decided to leave well alone. Let Leo sort out his own problems; she had her own.

Long before that week was over she knew herself hopelessly head over heels in love with the man she had married, yet his own emotions remained firmly under control. No matter how many times he made love to her he was always in full command of the situation, able to bring her to peak after peak of deliberately restrained pleasure before finally granting her release. She learned from him too, giving free rein to newly awakened instincts, delighting in her power to stir him at least this far. Physically they were perfect together; who was to say that one day they would not achieve a total union? It was something worth waiting for.

She looked at Morley with new eyes when she saw it again on the Friday afternoon Her home now—and her children's. Craig's children, she corrected herself with a faint wry smile. She was only the instrument.

Louise had tea ready and waiting in the drawing room. She welcomed them with open arms, her glance going from one face to the other with an air of satisfaction.

'You both look wonderful!' she smiled. 'That's what marriage does for you. Come and sit down and tell me what you thought of Inverness, Jessica. Did Craig take you to see my old home?'

'We never got there,' Jessica confessed, seeing no way out of it. 'The place outside Penrith was so good we decided to stay over.'

'Really?' The blue eyes held a sudden twinkle. 'Well, I suppose there wasn't much point in travelling further, especially considering you only had the week. Which reminds me, Craig, will you ring the office. I've had

Jake Loxley on the line three times already this afternoon—some crisis with the Middle East contract again, I gathered At any rate, he needs your word on it.'

'I'll do it now,' said Craig, and left the room.

There was sympathy in the gaze Louise returned to her daughter-in-law. 'Sorry about that, but I had to pass the message on. It sounded vital. Jake has apparently been trying to contact him for two days now in Inverness. You're very fortunate that no one knew the location of the place where you stayed.'

And even more so that Craig had not seen fit to advise his London office of his whereabouts, Jessica reflected. That particular piece of knowledge gave her a warm little glow of gratification. If she could make Craig forget about business matters there was hope for them yet.

The glow lasted only till his return. One look at his face was enough to tell her the worst.

'I have to go,' he said. 'If I leave at five I can be there by nine-thirty at the latest. Jake's setting up a meeting for first thing in the morning, gives me time to make the afternoon flight if it's deemed necessary. I hope to God it won't be. I've had enough of this fast and loose game they're playing.'

'I'll come and pack for you while you change,' offered Jessica, attempting to sound sensible and practical about it.

'Thanks.' He looked at her for a moment and seemed about to say something else, then obviously thought better of it, turning back to the door. 'Let's get to it.'

It took him little more than fifteen minutes to shower and shave and change from slacks and sweater into a suit. Jessica had the special lightweight carryall ready for him, with everything packed away in the zipped pockets in total preparation for any journey he might be called upon to undertake.

'Thanks,' he said again, taking it from her to sling it by its strap from one shoulder. 'That's been a big help.' He paused then, his eyes moving over her face with a closed expression. The shrug held resignation. 'It's just been one of those things you're going to have to get used to, I'm afraid. It goes with the job.'

Yours, or mine? she wondered. She forced a smile, keeping her tone deliberately light. 'I'll survive. Just take care, won't you?'

'Sure.' He made no attempt to kiss her goodbye, his mouth faintly twisted as if in recognition of the lacking element between them. 'I'll see you when I see you.'

Jessica saw him off from the outer doors, watching the Mercedes down the length of the drive and out of the gates before returning disconsolately to the drawing room where Louise waited with freshly brewed tea.

'It's a shame, I know,' said her mother-in-law sympathetically. 'Especially so soon. At least I never had that with his father. He was content to stay here and run the estate.'

'So it was Craig who brought in Bob Grainger?' hazarded Jessica in some surprise. 'I thought he'd been here a lot longer than that.'

Louise shook her head. 'He came a couple of months after James died. It was the first intimation I'd had that Craig didn't intend taking over the ropes himself on a permanent basis.' Her smile was just a little wry. 'You know Craig—act first and speak later! He's always been that way. I suppose I should be accustomed to it by now. Even where you were concerned, he never gave any hint of what he was thinking before springing it on me as a *fait accompli*. Not that I hadn't been hoping and praying it would eventually happen.'

'You just didn't expect it quite so soon,' Jessica finished for her. Her own smile held irony. 'You weren't the only one taken by surprise!'

'Still, it all worked out wonderfully well, didn't it?'

The question was purely rhetorical. 'Craig has a wife at last, and I have a companion. Why don't we take that trip to Whitby tomorrow if the fine weather holds? Sanders will drive us. You know, we really did make a lucky find with those two. Mrs Sanders runs the place like clockwork.'

Leaving me with what to do? reflected Jessica ruefully. One thing she was sure of, when children did come along there was going to be no nanny to take care of them. She would be doing that herself.

'Where's Beth?' she asked, more for something to say than from any idle curiosity.

'She went over to see Peter.' There was resignation in Louise's tone. 'I still can't see anything coming of it, but she has to make that decision herself. He obviously thinks a lot of her if he's willing to wait until she makes up her mind.'

'He loves her.' Jessica used the word softly, feeling the ache down deep. 'He always will.'

It was evening before she saw Leo. He was in the drawing room with a drink to hand when she went down prior to dinner.

'Hi, Sis,' was his typical greeting. 'How's marriage?'

'Marriage,' she said, 'is fine. How are things with you?'

He pulled a face. 'Same as usual, I suppose. Whatever changes are made around here they don't include me.'

'Stop feeling sorry for yourself,' Jessica chided lightly. 'If you're really so fed up do something concrete about it.'

'Such as what?'

'Sell the Ferrari, for a start. You said yourself it cost you a small fortune just to run.'

'You've been talking to Craig,' he accused. 'I asked you to put in a word, not ask him for advice.'

'I know that. I tried, but it didn't work.' She looked

at him a moment and sighed. 'Leo, you can't go through life expecting other people to fight your battles for you. If you went out and got yourself a job of some kind, and proved yourself capable of holding it down, Craig might very well be convinced enough to take you in with him. Anyway, it would be better than hanging around here kicking your heels against fate.'

He was studying her curiously, only half listening to what she was saying. 'You've changed,' he commented. 'You're starting to sound like Craig. Strange, that— you're the last person I'd have expected to subjugate herself to any man. Is that what love does for you?'

'Don't mock,' she retorted, avoiding his eyes. 'And don't run away with false impressions either. The relationship between Craig and myself is our business and no one else's.'

'Pardon me for breathing.' He gave a sudden short laugh. 'We're even rowing like brother and sister!'

'Then let's stop it now before it gets out of hand.' Jessica went to him, reaching up to plant a swift light kiss on his cheek. 'There. Friends again?'

'Of course.' There was an odd quality to his expression. 'I don't want to fall out with you, Jess.' He glanced at the carriage clock on the mantelpiece. 'What happened to Craig, anyway? I thought you'd come down together on your first night home.'

Jessica turned away to take a seat. 'He was called back to town, hadn't you heard?'

'Obviously not, or I wouldn't be asking. I only got in half an hour ago.' There was a pause before he added softly, 'I warned you what kind of wife he was looking for. You've only yourself to blame for marrying him.'

'I know that too.' She met his gaze with bland control. 'Would you like to pour me a sherry?'

'Sorry, I'm forgetting my manners.'

Louise came in while he was getting the drink, precluding any reopening of the subject on his part, but

Jessica knew it was not forgotten. If he knew the real truth he would be even more surprised at her, she reflected wryly. Not that she had any intention of telling him or anyone else what Craig really wanted a wife for.

Driving over the North Yorkshire moors to the little fishing port of Whitby was an experience to be remembered. Hill after rolling hill covered in gorse and heather, stretching to infinity.

Whitby itself she found a delight, the waterfront unspoiled by modern innovation, the narrow streets flanked by well-preserved dwellings, dating back a hundred years or more. High on the cliff overlooking the town stood the ruined Abbey, too exposed to the elements to withstand the passage of time, yet still a landmark for sailors along the coastline. Jessica climbed the many steps to view it at closer quarters, leaving Louise watching the fishermen mending their nets on the harbour side while she did so. From there she had the whole town spread beneath her, red roofs climbing up the steep banks from the quay, divided by the River Esk into two separate parts. Some time in the past Grandmother had stood here like this, she mused. Perhaps in this very spot. She had described the scene so well.

Later, after a picnic luncheon, they went to find Grape Lane and the home of Captain Cook, then visited a small workshop where craftsmen still produced items in the jet which had been so popular with the Victorians.

It was the first time that Jessica had realised jet was actually fossilised wood. Apparently it was to be found in the area in larger quantities than anywhere else in Britain. She bought a pendant set in silver on a finely linked chain, planning to give it to Beth, who had elected to stay at home today. A pair of beautifully worked cufflinks caught her eye too, but she studiously turned away. Craig had too many such things already. Why would he need any more?

They returned home around six to find a message to the effect that Craig was once again on his way east. Depression swamped Jessica as she looked ahead to see the pattern of her life spread before her. At least a child would give her something to think about other than herself.

There was no further communication the whole of that following week. But then there never was. To Craig business and home life were two totally separate entities, with little if any overlapping allowed. Jessica rode a lot with Beth and kept company with Louise in the evenings. With a whole library to go at she was hardly short of reading matter, yet she found it difficult these days to lose herself in a good book. What she needed was a regular occupation, but doing what? The house was run by Mrs Sanders. The most she herself was called upon to do was choose the day's menus, which hardly taxed mind or matter.

The phone call didn't come until Sunday evening. Craig sounded tired. 'I've just got in,' he said. 'I feel like sleeping for twenty-four hours straight through.'

'Then why don't you?' suggested Jessica, knowing what the answer would be. She hurried on before he could make it. 'How did it go?'

'The way it always goes. We appear to have it all on the level—until the next time. The Arabs have made an art of prevarication.' He pause, tone altering a little. 'What have you been doing with yourself?'

Missing you, she wanted to say, but couldn't find the courage. 'Not a lot,' she said instead. 'Have you any idea when you might make it home?'

'Maybe tomorrow, with any luck. Tuesday for certain.'

Providing nothing else cropped up between times. Jessica tried to keep any note of censure from her voice.

'Well, we can always hope. Thanks for letting me know you were back in the country.'

'The least I could do.' His own tone was abrupt. 'Goodnight, Jessica.'

She replaced the receiver slowly, aware of having handled that badly. Thanks for letting me know—as if he were some stranger instead of her husband. Why couldn't she let herself go and say the things she wanted to say, act the way she wanted to act? She knew why, of course. Pride, purely and simply. It was her besetting sin.

He arrived after lunch on Tuesday, coming out to the terrace where Jessica and Louise were relaxing over a final cup of coffee. It was purely for the latter's benefit that she made herself get up and go to kiss him, conscious of his lack of response.

'I'm only here for a couple of days,' Craig admitted, refusing to sit down on the plea of needing to change. 'Thursday I'm visiting the Birmingham plant. I'll probably stay the weekend and thrash out a few trouble spots with the G.M. Won't do him any harm to put in a little overtime.'

'You do far too much,' scolded his mother in the manner of one fully aware she was preaching a lost cause. 'I agree with Jessica. As chairman you should be in a position to sit back and let others bear the brunt.'

'A working chairman,' he corrected. The grey eyes hardened. 'Come on up and see what I've brought you back from Medina,' he added to Jessica.

It was more of a command than an invitation. She got up again without a word, donning a smile for Louise's sake. The carryall was in the hallway. Craig hoisted it on a shoulder to take upstairs with them, his expression aloof. Mounting the stairs at his side, Jessica searched her mind for some casual remark without success. Everything that had ever been between them had vanished at this moment.

There was a certain deliberation in the way he closed their suite door behind him. Letting the carryall drop to the floor, he came over to where she stood and pulled her roughly to him, his mouth finding hers with little tenderness about it.

'I've missed that,' he said, 'but I aim to make up for it. Get undressed.'

Colour flared in her face, then as swiftly faded again, leaving her pale but determined. 'If you're angry because of what your mother just said, tell me about it,' she demanded. 'Don't try to humiliate me this way!'

'You think it humiliating to go to bed with your own husband?' His brows were lifted mockingly. 'That doesn't sound like the girl I remember. She revelled in it!'

'Probably because the subject was approached with some degree of finesse,' she retorted. '"Get undressed" is hardly that!'

'All right,' he said, 'so I'll undress you. You have a beautiful body, Jessica. I want to see it and feel it when I make love to you. Anything wrong in that?'

'Making love doesn't cover what you have in mind.' The words were dragged from her. 'Why not be honest about it and use the proper term? I can take it.'

His eyes glittered suddenly and dangerously. 'Maybe I should show you the difference. It might teach you a thing or two.'

She bit her lip as he shed his jacket and started to unbuckle his belt, knowing him capable of carrying out the threat. The only way she was going to get out of this was by backing down and apologising for what she had said. It really had been going a bit too far, she had to admit.

'I take it back,' she proffered stiffly. 'You don't have to go to those lengths to teach me anything. I can imagine the difference.'

Craig had sat down on the bed edge to remove his

shoes. Fingers busy with the buttons of his shirt, he looked at her without visible signs of softening. 'Then why don't you do as I asked you to do and show some enthusiasm? It's why you married me, isn't it?'

Jessica sighed and began to take off her own clothing, wondering how she could love a man who would do this to her. Yet love him she did. She even understood him to a certain extent. This was his way of punishing her for not having had the pride and spirit to turn down the offer he had made her. Unfair, certainly, but she had known what she was taking on.

The anger in him faded once she was in his arms, giving way to a passion that carried her along with it. Opening her eyes in the aftermath of the storm, she found him watching her face with an unfathomable expression.

'You see,' he said softly, 'it's the same for us both. In this one way we have it all. What more is there?'

'Nothing,' she returned, steeling herself to match his mood. 'Like you said, we have it all. Do you really have to go away again on Thursday?'

'I'm afraid so. They're having union problems. It isn't going to be easy coming up with a policy acceptable to both parties. It never is. That's why I need the weekend. There's a meeting on Monday.' He dropped his head to put his lips to the pulse which beat faintly at her temple, smiling as she stirred beneath him. 'I'd take you with me, except that I'm going to be too tied up to pay you much attention. We'll just have to make the most of the time we have, won't we?'

Her senses sharpened again, brought back to life by the slow, subtle movement of his body, the feel of his lips against her skin. Right now nothing else mattered but the fact that he was here and they were together. Nothing!

CHAPTER TEN

THEY took the horses out on Wednesday afternoon, riding up on to the moors above and beyond the house to lose themselves in the wildness and solitude. Up here there was only the cry of the curlew to break the silence, the scent of warm grass and heather to fill the air. It was like being on another planet.

'Winter can be grim,' warned Craig practically when Jessica tried to impart something of her feelings to him. 'It's quite usual for the house to be cut off for whole days at a time.'

'How do you go about business matters then?' Jessica asked. 'By phone?'

'If I happen to be here at the time. In an emergency I'd call a helicopter to fetch me out—or in, as the case may be. The worst times are when the lines are down. Not that it happens too often, thank heaven.'

'It must have its compensations.' Jessica twisted in the saddle to look back over the swelling moorland the way they had come. 'Skiing, for instance?'

'Yes, we ski.' He looked at her with tolerance, taking in the brightness of her eyes under the hard hat brim, the colour in her skin. 'Do you?'

She shook her head regretfully. 'One more thing I never got round to, but I'd love to learn.'

'If you're as quick to pick that up as you've been in learning to ride we'll have you doing stem turns in no time,' he responded. 'You sit in the saddle as if you were born in it.'

'If blood really does mean anything perhaps I was.' She said it lightly, not looking at him. 'Have you forgiven me yet for not telling you the truth when I first arrived here?'

'I'm working on it.' Craig's tone was equally light. 'We'll stop here and give the horses a rest.'

They had come to the edge of the high plateau, looking out and down on a sweeping vista of broad green valley scattered with isolated farmhouses and stone-edged roads. A remaining section of crumbling dry stone wall in one of the closer fields looked like nothing so much as a giant alligator basking in the sun.

'Imagery,' Craig commented when Jessica pointed it out. 'I used to do it with cloud formations when I was a boy. In winter we light log fires to supplement the central heating. It's amazing what can be seen in red-hot embers.'

'Castles and dragons and fiery steeds,' she laughed, slipping to the ground and turning the gelding loose to graze. 'Of course it has to depend on temperament. I'll bet your images are far more realistic.'

'You mean prosaic.' He was smiling, but there was something else in his eyes. 'You could be right. I never was a romantic.'

He dropped at her side in the grass, leaning his back against the same rocky outcrop and bending a knee comfortably to rest an elbow. 'Beth's seeing Peter Turner again, isn't she?' he stated after a moment or two, on a different note. 'Did you have anything to do with that?'

'Not really.' She kept her face averted, her eyes on the black spot hovering in the sky. A hawk—or a kestrel; it was too far away to be sure. 'We talked about it a little.'

'With what conclusions?' He sounded lazy, almost disinterested, but Jessica knew him well enough by now to distrust that pose. 'I mean, what did you tell her?'

'That I didn't think she was ready to marry anybody yet but not to let that stop them from being friends.'

'Friends?' The question came soft.

'I doubt very much if they're lovers,' she said, still without looking at him. 'You'd know it with a girl like Beth.'

'You mean she looks untouched?' There was a certain irony in the inclination of the dark head. 'True, there's a particular aura about a woman when she's been with a man, only in her case it maybe doesn't show.'

'Then you'll just have to trust her, won't you?' This time she did turn her head towards him, eyes veiled. 'And Peter. He loves her far too much to risk hurting her in any way.'

The irony was still there in him. 'You're becoming quite a little mother confessor! Does Leo still confide in you too?'

'I don't mind lending an ear to anyone's problems,' she responded with control. 'Even where I can't offer much beyond sympathy.'

'You'd better not offer *anything* beyond sympathy,' he growled. 'To Leo or anyone else. When I said you could be your own mistress I meant exactly that.'

Jessica said tautly, 'You hardly leave me deprived, do you?'

'Not while I'm around.' He was unmoved by the jibe. 'And you're glad of it.'

She could hardly deny it. It was all that held them together. 'It's starting to cloud over,' she said, looking up at the sky. 'Shouldn't we be getting back?'

Craig reached for her arm as she made to push herself upright, drawing her round to face him. 'Are you regretting having married me?'

She gazed at him for a lengthy moment before answering, trying to read some deeper meaning into the words, but there was no flicker in the grey eyes. 'Would it make any difference if I was?' she said at last.

If there was a reaction at all it was not discernible.

'Not a lot,' Craig agreed, and let her go, getting to his feet to hold out a helping hand to assist her. 'You're right, it's time we were making tracks. It's going to rain.'

He made no attempt at conversation on the way back, concentrating on maintaining a good pace under the rapidly darkening sky. They were still a couple of miles short of the house when the rain began to fall, just a few large drops at first, then a sudden stinging shower settling into a steady downpour.

By the time they reached the stables they were both of them soaked to the skin, and Jessica was shivering. Leaving the horses in George's care, Craig took her straight across to the house and up to their room, striding into the bathroom to start a hot bath running.

'In there,' he ordered, 'and stay in until you're warmed right through. I'll have some hot tea brought up.'

She was lying in the water when he returned. Without looking at her, and quite without selfconsciousness, he stripped off his own sodden clothing and stepped into the shower cabinet, closing the door and turning on the tap full volume. Jessica could see the shape of him through the opaque glass, the tan of his body outlined against the white tiles. Had their relationship been closer to the normal kind between husband and wife, she might well have seen fit to join him under the shower: reaching up through the spray to kiss that firm yet yielding mouth, feeling his arms come about her, the water running over them both. She swallowed thickly. Craig would respond; she knew he would respond; he could no more help himself than she could. But it would be purely a physical union, because he knew no other kind.

So if that's all there is settle for it, she told herself fiercely and knew it was no use.

Craig left for Birmingham after breakfast. With the sun out again and the temperatures up in the seventies,

Jessica swam in the lake with Beth and took coffee out on the terrace, wondering how she was going to get through the weekend stretching ahead.

'I think I might pop across and see what I can do to help in the office,' she announced casually over lunch. 'If the Agency doesn't come up with somebody permanent soon Bob is going to wear himself out.'

'Craig won't like it,' Louise warned, then smiled. 'Not that you'll let that small factor deter you.'

Jessica didn't, making her way over as soon as she finished coffee. Bob was not yet back from his own lunch, his desk bearing indications of frustration in the way its contents had been scattered across the top of it as if by an impatient hand. Of Leo there was no sign. He had not been in to lunch either. Meeting Caroline's fiancé at the wedding had not helped matters, Jessica conceded, remembering the way he had looked—the defeat in his eyes. He might appear to have recovered his equilibrium on the surface, but she doubted if it was completely so. He kept his own counsel these days.

She had the desk into some semblance of order by the time Bob returned around two-thirty, the urgent items sorted for immediate attention, the rest neatly stacked. He didn't look too well, was her first thought on sight of him.

'Indigestion,' he admitted when she expressed some concern. 'Had it all night. Can't think what I might have eaten to cause it. Not as bad as this, anyway. It's like having a knife between the ribs!' He sat down behind the desk, viewing the tidied surface with lacklustre eyes. 'Not to appear ungrateful for a little help, but you know you shouldn't be here.'

'I don't have anything else to do,' she said mildly. 'Where's Leo, anyhow?'

Bob shook his head, the very movement weary. 'I haven't seen him since ten o'clock—said he had to go into Skipton. To be honest, he's not much help when he's here. No interest in the job. Do him the world of good to have to go out and fend for himself, that young man. Feckless, he is!'

Jessica was watching the slow, massaging movement of his hand as he attempted to relieve the discomfort a little 'Shouldn't you see a doctor?' she asked diffidently.

'For indigestion?' He sounded short. 'He'd think I'd gone soft! It'll go off in its own good time—always does.'

If he was prone to digestive problems he must know what he was talking about, Jessica reassured herself, but remained unconvinced. Any chest pain in a man his age was surely not to be ignored, even if it did turn out to be indigestion in the end. On the other hand, she could hardly insist that he saw a doctor.

He showed little inclination towards further conversation after that. Jessica busied herself with some government agricultural forms but found it difficult to concentrate on the officialese, listening instead to the laboured sound of Bob's breathing. He was in more discomfort than he was prepared to admit, she was sure of it. She wished Craig were at home. He would override the older man's wishes if he thought it necessary. Perhaps she should do that too—yet what right did she have?

She was still grappling with the problem when Leo came in some time later. He looked anything but happy.

'Get what you wanted?' asked Bob with unaccustomed sarcasm. 'It certainly took you long enough!'

'I had one or two things to see to.' Leo's tone was equally abrupt. 'I'm not bound to this place hand and foot!'

'You're not bound to it any way,' came the disgusted response. 'It just happens to be the one place where you can draw a fat salary for doing damned all!'

Leo's skin went dark red. 'I think you're outside your province, aren't you? Craig...'

'Craig wouldn't do anything to upset your mother, and well you know it. I'd go so far as to say you trade on it.' Bob was letting himself go in a manner Jessica had never witnessed before, his face suffused with anger, his whole bearing strained. 'How much longer are you going to go on being a parasite?'

'Bob!' It was a cry of entreaty from Jessica, her eyes fixed in concern on the heavy rise and fall of his chest, her ears tuned to the sound of agony in the rising note of his voice. 'You're not doing yourself...'

She was too late, of course. Even as she was speaking the ruddy colour drained from his face, one hand clutching his chest, his lips opening on a long, indrawn gasp as he fought to breathe. Leo was the nearest, but he made no move, rooted to the spot in horror-struck silence as though he couldn't believe what he was seeing. It was left to Jessica to leap forward to catch and support the suddenly slumping body in the chair, her heart thudding like a trip-hammer as she saw the already purpling lips.

'Help me get him on the floor!' she shouted to the still paralysed younger man. 'Leo!'

He came back to life with a jerk, stumbling round the desk to take the tweed-clad shoulders and ease the seemingly lifeless body out of the chair. Jessica went on her knees, putting her head down against Bob's chest to listen for a heartbeat. He had stopped breathing, but she could feel the faint flutter against her cheek. There was a chance yet, if only a slim one.

'Get an ambulance and a doctor,' she snapped over her shoulder, and shuffled hastily on her knees to seize the greying head and tilt it into the required position. She had only seen this done on film, never attempted it herself. A count of five between breaths, if she remembered correctly. Let it work, she prayed. Please let it work!

Seeing the chest inflate was a small miracle in itself, but it was only the beginning. An age seemed to pass before she felt the first voluntary intake and could afford to sit back on her heels to wipe the perspiration from her forehead. Bob's breathing was laboured, but he was at least breathing. She daren't look away in case he stopped again.

Leo came to kneel at her side, his face white as a sheet. 'It's on its way,' he said. 'I couldn't get any answer from the surgery, but he'll be in good hands with the emergency team. How is he doing?'

'He's alive,' said Jessica, 'but only just. How long are they going to be?'

'They said fifteen minutes. It's a specially equipped cardiac unit. If only he can hang on.'

As if in answer to that last, Bob's eyelids fluttered open and a low groan escaped from his lips. He looked at the two faces bending over him with confused expression.

'Don't talk,' said Jessica urgently, as he half opened his mouth. 'You've had a heart attack, but there's help on the way.'

'Can't breathe.' The words were a painful whisper of sound. 'Chest hurts!'

Jessica took a hasty look around the office. 'I think he should be propped up a little to ease the pressure.' She pointed to an upright chair. 'Fetch that, Leo, and turn it on its end so the back forms a ramp. Then I'll need your jacket and the squab out of the desk chair.'

Leo fetched the items and helped her arrange them, then between them they slowly and gently slid the chair back beneath the invalid's lifted shoulders until he was resting at an angle to the floor. Bob made no attempt to speak again, but it was obvious that he found the new position a little easier.

'Shall you be okay if I slip across and let Mother know what's happening?' asked Leo hesitantly. 'If she looks out and sees the ambulance coming up the drive she's liable to get too much of a shock herself.'

'Of course,' Jessica agreed. 'It's a good thing you thought about it.'

The shake of his head was rueful. 'It's probably my fault it happened at all. I knew he wasn't feeling too good this morning, but I still went off and left him to it.' He got to his feet before she could reply. 'Shan't be long.'

The seconds seemed like hours after he had gone. Bob's eyes were closed again, his breathing shallow, his colour grey. Whatever happened he would obviously not be taking on the full responsibility of the job again, which posed a question for the future. Not that it mattered one iota right now. If only the ambulance would come!

The sound of hurrying feet lifted her head. Peter came swiftly into the office closely followed by Beth.

'I've just arrived,' he said. 'Leo told us what had happened. Let me have a look at him, Jessica.'

She was only too glad to relinquish her position, getting stiffly to her feet to meet Beth's concerned eyes with a faint smile. 'He'll be fine now.'

The ambulance arrived soon after that. With the patient aboard and on oxygen, Peter took a brief moment to speak to the two girls.

'I'm going in with him. Beth, will you contact Dad at the Morrisons' and ask him to take evening surgery for me if I don't get back in time?'

She nodded, eyes dark but filled with a kind of resolution. 'I'll go and break the news to Margaret too,' she offered. 'She'll take it better from someone she knows. I'll bring her to the hospital, shall I?'

'If you think she's up to it.' His smile was reassuring. 'I'll leave it to your judgment.'

It seemed very quiet after the ambulance had left.

'Do you want me to come with you?' asked Jessica as Beth turned towards the estate car parked nearby.

The younger girl shook her head. 'Better if I handle it on my own. Margaret suffers from a nervous complaint, but she's used to me. I call and see her two or three times a week.'

Jessica let her go, returning to the house to find Louise. Leo was still with her in the drawing room.

'We were just contemplating whether to call Craig now or leave it until we know more,' he said. 'Mother thinks he should be told.'

'I agree.' Jessica looked at her mother-in-law with some anxiety, taking in the lack of colour in her face. 'Are you all right?'

'It's been a shock,' the other woman admitted. 'Who would have thought this was going to happen— although I'd noticed Bob was looking rather tired recently. I put it down to worry over Margaret. She's been a terrible trial to him these last few years. She suffers from agoraphobia. It must be almost three years since she went any farther than the garden gate. Did anyone go to tell her?'

Jessica nodded. 'Beth did.'

'Beth?' Louise sounded surprised. 'I shouldn't have thought her the best person for that job!'

'Apparently she thought so. She even insisted on going alone.' Jessica moved suddenly and decisively towards the phone. 'I'm going to try to reach Craig. At least I can leave a message.'

Getting through to the Birmingham factory was no problem at all, getting to speak to Craig himself something else again. It took perseverance on Jessica's part before she was finally connected. His voice sounded brusque over the line.

'Jessica? What is it? I'm in a meeting.'

Her explanation was succinct and concise. He was silent for a moment after she finished speaking.

'I'll give you a number to ring as soon as you hear from the hospital,' he said at length. 'They'll pass on any message.'

'You're not coming back?' The question was torn from her.

'I'm trying to avert a strike down here,' came the clipped response. 'Just keep me advised. Do you have a pencil handy?'

Jessica took down the number he gave her without further comment, composing her features as she replaced the receiver and turned to face the other two.

'We're to let him know what happens.'

Louise spread her hands in a gesture that was almost defensive. 'Well, I don't suppose there's anything he could do if he did come home.'

'Life goes on.' Leo made no attempt to disguise his own feelings on the matter. 'I hope he isn't expecting me to take over Bob's job on my own.'

'I'll help,' offered Jessica before his mother could speak. 'The two of us should be able to cope until something is sorted out. When Craig gets back . . .' She broke off there, unable to see beyond that time. 'Well, we'll have to wait,' she finished lamely.

It was after six before Peter phoned through from the hospital to say that Bob was out of immediate danger and responding to treatment. It had been a severe attack, he added, and recovery was going to take time.

Jessica rang the number Craig had given her but was unable to speak with him personally, although she was assured that the message would be passed on at the earliest opportunity. Under the circumstances he would probably see little need to hurry home, she acknowledged dully. One problem at a time, was Craig's maxim.

Louise elected to take dinner in her own rooms that evening, leaving Jessica and Leo to dine alone as Beth had not yet returned. Her brother-in-law had something on his mind, she judged, viewing him across the table. He looked the same way he had looked on his return from Skipton earlier, before Bob's collapse had taken precedence.

'Do you want to talk about it?' she asked softly at length, unable to stand the long silence. 'It sometimes helps.'

The shrug and negative movement of the dark head lacked conviction. 'I can't involve you, Jess. It wouldn't be fair.'

'You obviously need to involve someone,' she said, registering the unspoken plea. 'Try me.'

He eyed her for a lengthy moment without speaking, blue eyes devoid of sparkle. 'Don't you have problems of your own?'

'Don't we all?' she countered smoothly. 'That doesn't mean we don't have room to sympathise with others.'

His smile held a wry quality. 'I doubt if you'll feel much sympathy with my particular one.' He paused then, glance sliding away to the silver candelabrum in front of her. 'It's Deirdre. She thinks she could be pregnant.'

Jessica could find no immediate comment—none, at least, that seemed adequate. Recalling the pretty young face of the girl in question she felt a sudden stirring of anger. This was taking a lack of responsibility too far!

'I thought you'd broken things off,' she murmured at length, realising even as she said it how totally irrelevant the comment was.

Leo's reply confirmed the view. 'Not soon enough.'

'So what are you going to do about it?'

'I don't know,' he admitted. 'I honestly don't know.' He paused, eyes coming back to her face. 'You wouldn't suggest I married her?'

'Not if you don't love her. You've already gone most of the way to ruining her life. There's no point in compounding mistakes' She was unable to keep the censure from her voice. 'Leo, she's only seventeen!'

'Eighteen. She had a birthday a couple of weeks ago.' He sounded defensive. 'I thought you'd understand.'

'Oh, I do. I understand perfectly. You took advantage of a total infatuation. The way she obviously felt about you she'd have jumped off a cliff if you'd told her to!'

'It takes two,' he muttered.

'Physically, perhaps. Emotionally you have to be streets ahead.' She made a gesture towards him as he threw down his napkin and started to rise. 'Don't run away. You're going to have to take a whole lot more than I can dish out when her family gets to know—to say nothing of your own.'

He subsided again, resignation written across the handsome features. 'All right, so I deserve everything I get. What I need now is some constructive advice.'

'I'm not sure I'm the right person to give it,' said Jessica carefully. 'Your mother . . .'

'I'd rather keep her out of it.'

'She's going to have to know some time.'

'Not necessarily. Not if it turns out to be a false alarm. Deirdre only says she thinks she might be. Perhaps she's just trying to scare me into something.' He met her gaze again and flushed. 'It could be. She didn't want to accept that I wouldn't be seeing her again. She wouldn't be the first to try this routine.'

'You really think she's capable of that kind of subterfuge?'

'I'm not sure. All I know is she told several people we were going to be married.'

'With absolutely no justification?'

'None.' There was a pause, then he gave a faint sigh. 'Well, at least I never mentioned the word marriage.'

'Just gave her enough cause to believe there was a future for you both.'

'Not that either. Not in so many words.' Leo spread

his hands helplessly. 'It only happened once, Jess. I didn't even plan it. The car . . .'

'Spare me the details.' Her tone was brusquer than she had intended. She made some attempt to soften it. 'When are you seeing her again?'

'Tonight. I'm picking her up outside the cinema at nine-thirty.'

'Isn't that rather late?'

'The show doesn't finish till around ten-fifteen. That gives us about an hour to talk before she's expected home. I had to promise I'd be there, Jess. She was close to being hysterical about it this afternoon.'

'What are you going to say to her?'

'Lord only knows! Even if it were a certainty I still couldn't tell her what she wants to hear. She's a sweet kid, but I don't want to be tied down that way.'

Jessica said dryly, 'I doubt if you're really what she needs either.'

'Then come with me and tell her that, will you?' There was entreaty in his voice. 'Please, Jess! I don't think I can face her on my own again.'

All in all, Jessica decided resignedly, it might be better for Deirdre if he didn't. Pushed too far, there was no telling what a girl in her state might do. 'All right,' she said, 'I'll come. I'm not sure what I can do to help, but at least I can try.'

'Thanks!' He was patently relieved. 'You're a gem, Jess. Craig doesn't know how lucky he is!'

There was no answer to that. Where Craig was concerned, Jessica thought painfully, luck played little part.

CHAPTER ELEVEN

THEY took the other estate car, reaching the cinema right on the half hour to find Deirdre already waiting. Jessica had taken a rear seat. It wasn't until the younger girl was actually in the car that she even realised anyone else was present.

Leo set off before she had chance to jump out again, taking the main route out of town. 'You've met my sister-in-law,' he said. 'She thought she might be able to help.'

'You've told her?' Deirdre sounded dismayed, as if the very thought of anyone else knowing her secret was anathema to her. 'Leo, you shouldn't have! If my father gets to know...'

'He won't hear it from me,' Jessica put in reassuringly. 'Nobody will. Leo simply didn't know what else to do, that's all.'

'It doesn't have anything to do with anyone else.' The other girl didn't appear to be listening, her eyes fixed on Leo's face with heartrending appeal. 'You had no right!'

'I'm sorry.' He was obviously at a total loss for anything else to say. 'Like Jess says, I didn't know what else to do. You gave me a real shock this afternoon. I couldn't even think straight.'

'You don't want me.' Her voice was very small, the big brown eyes suddenly losing all life. 'Even with this you still don't want me, do you, Leo?'

'I don't want either of us doing something we're going to regret.' The words were forced from him. 'I'd make a rotten husband.'

'No, you wouldn't!' She came alive again with a

vehemence surprising in one so slight of stature, long dark hair falling forward about her face as she reached out to catch at his arm. 'I wouldn't care, anyway!'

'You would. You'd hate me for it.' Leo was wretched, searching desperately for ways to say what he had to say. 'We'd finish up hating each other.'

'Leo,' Jessica spoke quietly but with some authority, conscious of the need to make some definite move, 'do you think you could find a place to stop the car where we could talk without interruption?'

'I won't talk to *you* about anything!' Deirdre flung at her, half turning in her seat. 'It's between me and Leo and nobody else!' Her face crumpled suddenly, her head going down to the seat back as tears overflowed. 'I wish I were dead!'

Leo had switched into a quiet side street. Pulling up on a corner, he killed the engine and sat looking helplessly at the sobbing figure at his side. 'Jess,' he appealed.

'Go for a walk,' she said. 'Don't come back for at least fifteen minutes.'

He went with alacrity, obviously thankful to be out of the line of fire even for a short time. Jessica made no attempt to touch the younger girl, waiting until the sobs dwindled to sniffs before proffering a wad of tissue.

'I always carry these for emergencies,' she said. 'Take your time. We can always send Leo away again if he comes back too soon.'

'I don't want him to go away.' The words were muffled. 'What gives you the right to push your nose in, anyway?'

'Leo asked me,' Jessica responded. 'I can't say I was too keen on the idea either, but he didn't know how to handle the situation.'

'And you do?'

'Let's just say I'm better equipped than he is.' She paused, letting the silence ride for a moment or two before adding softly, 'Is it true, Deirdre?'

'Is what true?' She still hadn't lifted her head.

'You know what I mean. Are you pregnant?'

It seemed doubtful at first that she was even going to get an answer. She was on the verge of repeating the question when Deirdre stirred, lifting a woebegone little face stained with tears.

'It doesn't make any difference now, does it?'

'It makes a lot of difference.' Jessica tried hard to keep her voice unemotional. 'More to you than anyone. You can get over losing Leo, but a baby is something else.'

'I wanted it.' The tears had dried now, but they weren't far away. 'I really wanted it to be true.'

'Only it isn't.'

'No.' There was a bitter little note of defeat in the admission. 'I thought it might be for a few days, but it wasn't. It wouldn't have been any use, anyway, would it?'

'I'm afraid not.' Jessica said it as gently as she was able. 'Naturally Leo wouldn't have left you to manage on your own, but he isn't ready to marry anyone. This way at least makes things easier.'

'Lets him off the hook, you mean.' Spite took a brief upper hand. 'My father would kill him if he knew what he'd done!'

'Except that he'd have to know what you'd done too,' Jessica pointed out, hating herself for it, 'and if he's the kind of man I think he is he'll have very definite views on his daughter's behaviour. Am I right?'

The sigh came long and deep. 'Yes. He'd half kill me too. He doesn't even know I've been going with Leo. He wouldn't like it if he did.'

'Then be thankful you don't have to tell him.' Jessica put out an impulsive hand and touched the dark head. 'Deirdre, I understand how you feel about Leo, really I do. He's a very attractive man. Only you'll get over it, I can vouch for that. One of these days you'll meet someone else who'll make you wonder what on earth you saw in Leo Stafford!' She caught the sudden alteration in the other girl's expression and smiled wryly. 'Well, all right, so perhaps you'll always hold a memory of him. First love is a bit special.'

Curiosity momentarily overcame resentment. 'You mean your husband isn't the first man you've been in love with?'

It was a difficult question to answer. Jessica took her time in doing so, aware that she owed the girl honesty at least. 'He's the first man I've loved in quite the same way,' she said at length. 'When you fall in love again it will probably be a totally different feeling from now with Leo.'

'Better?'

'Very much so if he loves you back.' She blanked off the thought before it could take hold. This was not the time to be thinking of her own problems.

Leo was coming back, his approach tentative as if he half expected to be waved away again. Deirdre turned her head away when he got into the car.

'I want to go home,' she said.

They dropped her at the top of her road, watching her safely indoors before driving on. She had made no farewells, lips pressed tightly together, eyes averted as she got out of the car. Leo drew a sigh of relief when they finally moved away.

'I don't know how you did it,' he said, 'but thanks. I'm assuming I don't have anything to worry about after all?'

'Apart from breaking the girl's heart, not a thing.' Jessica's tone was heavy with irony.

The shrug failed to disguise discomfiture. 'She'll get over it.'

'Oh yes, she will. Only not right away, and not that easily. You've hurt her very badly, Leo.'

'All right, don't rub it in.' He sounded rueful. 'I've been lucky to get off so lightly.' He paused, his tone changing a little. 'All the same, I'd like to know how she imagined pretending to be pregnant was going to help. Even if I'd been willing to do the right thing, so to speak, she could hardly have kept up that kind of deception for long.'

'Lack of foresight. You should know plenty about that.' Jessica saw no reason to let him off easily. 'Stick to your own weight in future, will you, Leo?'

'I would, except that they all keep up and marrying other men.'

The flippancy was all on the surface. Jessica knew a sudden pang of sympathy. 'I'm sorry about Caroline. Sorry for you, I mean. You were obviously never destined to come together.'

His glance slid briefly sideways as they pulled up for traffic lights. 'You think you and Craig were?'

Her throat closed up, making her voice sound husky. 'It would seem that way, wouldn't it? Just imagine the sheer coincidence of my turning up at the very time you happened to be looking for a replacement for Miss Branston.'

'The unwitting instrument of fate,' Leo agreed dryly, putting his foot down on the amber light to get ahead of the vehicle on his right. 'Not exactly the ideal partnership, though, is it? You've barely seen him since you got back from your honeymoon. He won't change, you realise. Not now.'

'I wouldn't expect him to change.' She was hard put to it to stop herself from saying something hard and cutting. 'Believe it or not, I married him without any illusions.'

'For love?'

'For love.' She used the word with deliberation.

'Well, I only hope he appreciates it. He certainly does little enough to deserve it!'

'How would you know?' she flashed. 'You don't know him, Leo. You never did! How do you think you might react to the load of responsibility he was landed with at your age? Could you take the place of a father to a thirteen-year-old without making some mistakes? Perhaps his biggest one was in not beating some common sense into that thick head of yours. It might have taught you to stop and think about the consequences before seducing seventeen-year-old girls, if nothing else!' She stopped there, biting her lip. 'I'm sorry,' she offered on a more controlled note. 'That was nasty.'

'But true.' Leo sounded rueful. 'I'm totally responsible.'

He was silent after that, and Jessica was content to leave it. The day had been long and fraught and she wished it could be over. Tomorrow, with any luck, Craig might return. How he would tackle the problems she had little idea, except to be pretty sure of his refusal to countenance her own participation in estate management. A new man would be a first priority, it was to be hoped with provision for Bob to return on a part-time basis should the latter prove able. In the meantime, Leo was simply going to have to pull his weight, for once.

It was almost a quarter past eleven by the time they reached the house. They left the car in the yard and went in via the rear entrance. Lights still blazed despite the quietness of the place. Jessica wondered if Beth was back yet and how she had coped with Margaret Grainger. Her whole attitude had been so determined, as if she needed to prove something to herself as much as others.

Leo caught her up at the foot of the stairs, taking her elbow to turn her back towards him. There was no flippancy about him now. He looked and sounded totally sincere.

'Jess, you've been wonderful. I don't know what I'd have done without you.' He paused, eyes searching her face, and added gruffly, 'Craig really doesn't realise how lucky he is!'

'On the contrary,' came the grim interruption from the drawing-room doorway, 'Craig knows exactly how lucky he is!'

Leo was the first to speak, tone wry. 'Whatever you're thinking it isn't the way it looks.'

'No?' The word held a wealth of irony. 'Then supposing you tell me where the hell you've been?'

It was Jessica who answered this time. 'Solving a minor problem. What time did you get back?'

'Half an hour ago.' His expression hadn't altered. 'What kind of problem?'

'One of mine,' said Leo before she could answer. 'It needn't involve you.'

His brother's jaw tightened ominously. 'I think anything that involves my wife automatically involves me. Supposing the two of you come in here and tell me about it.'

'No!' Jessica spoke sharply to conceal the faint tremor in her voice. 'Leo's right, Craig. It's over, and best forgotten.'

The grey eyes held a steely glint. 'I want to know where you've been. Otherwise I'll assume you're both of you covering up.'

'Can you still love a man who trusts you the way he trusts you?' asked Leo in disgust, watching Jessica's face. 'He doesn't deserve you, you know that.'

'I'm not sure who deserves what,' she responded on a dull note. 'I'm going to bed.'

Both men watched her mount the stairs without moving from their relative positions. Only when she was in the bathroom with the door closed did Jessica relax the iron control. Leo had asked a valid question back there. Could she still love a man who would think her capable of having an affair with his own brother?

Not only could, but did, she was bound to acknowledge. Otherwise it wouldn't hurt this way. If she could only imagine that Craig's own feelings on the subject went any deeper than mere pride it would be something.

She was brushing her hair at the dressing table when he finally came into the room. He stood just within the doorway looking across at her, an odd expression on his face.

'Did you find out what you wanted to know?' she asked, laying down the brush with an unsteady hand.

'I'm not sure,' he admitted, and for the first time she heard uncertainty in his voice. 'Jessica, will you answer me one question honestly?'

Her shoulders moved in a gesture which betrayed her weariness. 'If I can.'

'Do you love me?' The words were quietly spoken but with a curious inflection.

She went very still, eyes fixed on his image through the mirror. This tall, dark enigmatic man was both husband and lover; he knew every inch of her body the way she knew his, yet their minds were as far apart as ever. She didn't know why he was asking what he was asking because he wouldn't let her in even now. Yet one of them had to make the move.

'Yes,' she said, 'I do. I'm sorry if it goes beyond what you wanted from me, but I don't have control over my emotions the way you do.'

'The way I thought I did.' His voice was soft, gentler than at any other time she had heard it. 'I wanted you the first time we met, Jessica, but you wouldn't let me leave it at that. You got under my guard the way no other woman ever did.'

He came over to where she still sat gazing at him,

drawing her to her feet and turning her towards him. The grey eyes were warmed by a light she had longed to see there, his hands tender. 'I had to hear you say it first. I never could be sure of your feelings before. Sometimes you've looked at me as if you hated me.'

'Sometimes I've felt that way,' she confessed. 'They're closely allied emotions, I believe.' She paused, still unable to see very far beyond the façade. 'You haven't used the word to me yet. Is it so difficult?'

He smiled then, his whole face taking on a totally new look. 'It might have been once, but not any more. I love you, Jessica. I can't bear to be away from you. When I am I feel incomplete. Does that answer your question?'

'Partially,' she acknowledged, 'but not wholly.' Her voice tremoured a little. 'Make love to me, Craig. Make love to me with love. There is a difference.'

'There's a difference in knowing how you really feel.' His eyes were kindling, passion flaring swiftly. He slid the thin straps of her nightdress from her shoulders, allowing the garment to slide to the floor, his hands following its passage down over the smooth curves of her body. 'You're so lovely. I dream about doing this. Titian hair and skin like Devon cream. It's the most stirring combination known to man!'

She clung to him as he lifted and carried her to the bed, lips warm against his neck. Only when he put her down did she open her eyes, a sudden new light dawning in them.

'No,' she said softly, 'this time it's my turn. Just for once, Craig, let me be the lover and you the recipient. I can show the way I feel much better than I can tell you.'

For a moment there was doubt in his eyes, but it faded as she drew him down beside her. She removed his clothing with deftness, pausing to kiss him between times; smiling at the bemused expression on his face. Stripped he was magnificent, long and lean and hard-muscled, his skin deeply tanned everywhere but for the narrow line about his hips. He needed no further arousal for sure, but she was not yet ready to return him to control.

She began at his feet, kissing each of his toes with butterfly strokes of her lips, working her way slowly and gradually up the full length of his body until she finally lay stretched along him to find his mouth in a deep, endless searching for the man within.

'Oh, God, Jessica,' he groaned when she at last lifted her mouth from his, 'where have you been all my life?'

'Waiting for you,' she murmured. 'Just waiting for you.'

Her hair had fallen forward over her face, covering them both like a cloak. Her eyes asked a question, looking deep into his, reading the answer even as he took her by the shoulders and turned her beneath him with one powerful surge of his body.

'Not yet,' he said. 'I'm not prepared. Maybe I never will be. Can you understand that?'

'Of course.' She put her hands either side of the strong face, loving every line. 'I don't want to take anything away from you, Craig. I love you the way you are. My own, dominant male!'

Jessica awoke at first light still wrapped in his arms, content to lie still despite the cramp in her legs and watch his sleeping face for a moment or two. Was there really a softer look about those angular features, she wondered, or was it just that she could see him now with new eyes? Last night had been unforgettable; a total merging of spirit and flesh earth-shattering in its effect. How would it be when Craig went away again, as he inevitably must? Not just his lovemaking but his very presence was essential to her everyday life.

As if in response to a signal, his own eyes opened, realisation dawning slowly as they looked into hers.

'It's true,' he said. 'I thought I'd been dreaming again. What . . .'

She closed his mouth with a kiss, feeling him stir to immediate life against her with a sense of exultation that she could arouse him as swiftly and easily as this. If their time together was to be limited then they must make the most of it. Day or night. What did it matter? She wanted him, wanted him, *wanted* him!

They were both of them showered and dressed before she got around to asking the question to which she dreaded the answer.

'How long will you be home?'

'That's something we have to discuss seriously,' he said, fastening the last button of his shirt. 'With Bob out of action things around here have to undergo some changes, for sure.'

'You mean you'll have to find a temporary manager to take over?'

Craig looked at her then, decisiveness in the line of his mouth. 'I mean I'm going to take over the estate myself from now on. Bob can help out to his own capabilities as soon as he's able.'

Jessica's heart was beating fast enough to hurt, but she dared not allow herself to believe what she was hearing. 'For good?' she got out.

The grey eyes were steady though not without regret. 'For good. I don't pretend to view the prospect with total delight, but it's time I started taking stock of my own responsibilities. Morley means more to me in the long run than any of my business commitments.' His voice softened suddenly. 'And you mean more than all of them put together.'

Jessica went to him, putting her arms about his neck

to lay her cheek against his with a small, deep sigh of relief. 'Craig, life won't be boring, I promise you that. When your son is born we'll both wish there were more than twenty-four hours in the day.'

'My son?' He held her away from him, searching her face with new enlightenment. 'Are you sure?'

'As sure as I can be without medical confirmation.' She smiled a little. 'It's as much a feeling as anything else—I know it's there. Aren't you pleased?'

'I'm not sure,' he admitted. 'It was what I wanted, but that was before all this. Now . . .' he paused, lifting his shoulders with a faint wry smile . . . 'I'm going to have to share you too soon.'

'Never,' she promised him. 'I'll never be that kind of mother. We'll share the baby. He won't come between us in any fashion.'

His kiss was hard and fierce. 'Nothing will!'

Going downstairs, Jessica said tentatively, 'What about Leo, Craig? You know he'll never settle down here. Can't you find him something?'

'I'm thinking about it,' he conceded. 'Especially after what I got out of him last night.' His glance flicked sideways, taking in her expression with a slant of his lips. 'He's lucky he had you to fall back on. The girl could have brought him a whole lot of trouble. Is she going to be all right?'

'As well as any other eighteen-year-old who's lost her virginity to a man who didn't love her.' Jessica shook her head. 'It's one of those things no one can do much about. She's terrified of her father finding out. She'll get over it in time, of course.'

'But it would certainly help if Leo was removed from the scene altogether.' Craig paused on the bottom step, a hand on the newel post, resignation in his eyes. 'So I find him something. Only he's going to do some compromising himself, I can tell you! The Ferrari goes, for one thing!'

Jessica could barely contain her delight. Everything was working out. There would be times, she knew, when Craig would miss his former life, but she would make it up to him. She had the power, she had the ability, she had the love.

ROMANCE

Variety is the spice of romance

Each month, Mills & Boon publish new romances. New stories about people falling in love. A world of variety in romance – from the best writers in the romantic world. Choose from these titles in April.

AN ELUSIVE DESIRE Anne Mather
SUP WITH THE DEVIL Sara Craven
ONE WHO KISSES Marjorie Lewty
ONE MORE TIME Karen van der Zee
A MOUNTAIN FOR LUENDA Essie Summers
PHANTOM MARRIAGE Penny Jordan
CAPTIVE LOVING Carole Mortimer
MASTER OF MORLEY Kay Thorpe
SOMEWHERE TO CALL HOME Kerry Allyne
DARK SEDUCTION Flora Kidd
SECOND TIME AROUND Elizabeth Oldfield
THE TYCOON'S LADY Kay Clifford

On sale where you buy paperbacks. If you require further information or have any difficulty obtaining them, write to: Mills & Boon Reader Service, PO Box 236, Thornton Road, Croydon, Surrey CR9 3RU, England.

Mills & Boon
the rose of romance

Best Seller Romances

These best loved romances are back

Mills & Boon Best Seller Romances are the love stories that have proved particularly popular with our readers. These are the titles to look out for this month.

WILD MELODY Sara Craven
BLUEGRASS KING Janet Dailey
SECRETARY WIFE Rachel Lindsay
THE MEDICI LOVER Anne Mather
THE WHISPERING GATE Mary Wibberley
TIME OF THE TEMPTRESS Violet Winspear

Buy them from your usual paperback stockist, or write to: Mills & Boon Reader Service, P.O. Box 236, Thornton Rd, Croydon, Surrey CR9 3RU, England. Readers in South Africa write to: Mills & Boon Reader Service of Southern Africa, Private Bag X3010, Randburg, 2125.

Mills & Boon
the rose of romance

ROMANCE

Next month's romances from Mills & Boon

Each month, you can choose from a world of variety in romance with Mills & Boon. These are the new titles to look out for next month.

DESIRE'S CAPTIVE Penny Jordan
FEVER PITCH Sarah Holland
CANDLEGLOW Amii Lorin
THE MARRIAGE CONTRACT Susan Alexander
CLOSEST PLACE TO HEAVEN Lynsey Stevens
DREAM OF MIDSUMMER Catherine George
MOMENT OF MADNESS Patricia Lake
LIONS WALK ALONE Susanna Firth
FANTASY GIRL Carole Mortimer
STORMY WEATHER Sandra Clark
INTIMATE ENEMIES Jessica Steele
THE SLENDER THREAD Yvonne Whittal

Buy them from your usual paperback stockist, or write to: Mills & Boon Reader Service, P.O. Box 236, Thornton Rd, Croydon, Surrey CR9 3RU, England. Readers in South Africa write to: Mills & Boon Reader Service of Southern Africa, Private Bag X3010, Randburg, 2125.

Mills & Boon
the rose of romance

Masquerade Historical Romances

From the golden days of romance

Picture the days of real romance – from the colourful courts of mediaeval Spain to the studied manners of Regency England. Masquerade Historical romances published by Mills & Boon vividly recreate the past. Look out for these superb new stories this month.

LADY OF THE MOON
Alex Andrews

THE LAST MISS LYNTON
Ann Edgeworth

Buy them from your usual paperback stockist, or write to: Mills & Boon Reader Service, P.O. Box 236, Thornton Rd, Croydon, Surrey CR9 3RU, England. Readers in South Africa – write to: Mills & Boon Reader Service of Southern Africa, Private Bag X3010, Randburg, 2125.

Mills & Boon
the rose of romance

Doctor Nurse Romances

Romance in the wide world of medicine

Amongst the intense emotional pressures of modern medical life, doctors and nurses often find romance. Read about their lives and loves in the three fascinating Doctor Nurse romances, available this month.

FIRST-YEAR'S FANCY
Lynne Collins

DESERT FLOWER
Dana James

INDIAN OCEAN DOCTORS
Juliet Shore

Mills & Boon
the rose of romance

FREE – an exclusive Anne Mather title, MELTING FIRE

At Mills & Boon we value very highly the opinion of our readers. What <u>you</u> tell us about what you like in romantic reading is important to us.

So if you will tell us which Mills & Boon romance you have most enjoyed reading lately, we will send you a copy of MELTING FIRE by Anne Mather – absolutely FREE.

There are no snags, no hidden charges. It's absolutely FREE.

Just send us your answer to our question, and help us to bring you the best in romantic reading.

CLAIM YOUR FREE BOOK NOW

Simply fill in details below, cut out and post to: Mills & Boon Reader Service, FREEPOST, P.O. Box 236, Croydon, Surrey CR9 9EL.

The Mills & Boon story I have most enjoyed during the past 6 months is:

TITLE _____

AUTHOR _____ BLOCK LETTERS, PLEASE

NAME (Mrs/Miss) _____ EP4

ADDRESS _____

_____ POST CODE _____

Offer restricted to ONE Free Book a year per household. Applies only in U.K. and Eire.
CUT OUT AND POST TODAY – NO STAMP NEEDED.

Mills & Boon
the rose of romance